Stitched Together

a quilting cozy

Carol Dean Jones

C&T PUBLISHING

Text copyright © 2018
by Carol Dean Jones

Photography and artwork copyright
© 2018 by C&T Publishing, Inc.

Publisher: Amy Marson

Creative Director: Gailen Runge

Acquisitions Editor: Roxane Cerda

Managing Editor: Liz Aneloski

Project Writer: Teresa Stroin

Technical Editor / Illustrator:
Linda Johnson

Cover/Book Designer: April Mostek

Production Coordinator:
Zinnia Heinzmann

Production Editor: Jennifer Warren

Photo Assistant: Mai Yong Vang

Cover photography by Lucy Glover and
Mai Yong Vang of C&T Publishing, Inc.

Cover quilt: *Stitched Together*, 2014,
by the author

Library of Congress Cataloging-in-
Publication Data

Names: Jones, Carol Dean, author.

Title: Stitched together : a quilting cozy /
Carol Dean Jones.

Description: Lafayette, California :
C&T Publishing, [2018] | Series:
A quilting cozy series ; book 5

Identifiers: LCCN 2018003526 |
ISBN 9781617457449 (softcover)

Subjects: LCSH: Quilting--Fiction. |
Retirees--Fiction. | Retirement
communities--Fiction. | GSAFD:
Mystery fiction.

Classification: LCC PS3610.O6224 S75
2018 | DDC 813/.6--dc23

LC record available at
https://lccn.loc.gov/2018003526

Printed in the USA

10 9 8 7 6 5 4 3 2 1

A Quilting Cozy Series

by Carol Dean Jones

Left Holding the Bag (book 10)

Tattered & Torn (book 9)

Missing Memories (book 8)

The Rescue Quilt (book 7)

Moon Over the Mountain (book 6)

Stitched Together (book 5)

Patchwork Connections (book 4)

Sea Bound (book 3)

Running Stitches (book 2)

Tie Died (book 1)

Acknowledgments

My sincere appreciation goes out to my special friends: Phyllis Inscoe, Janice Packard, Sharon Rose, and Barbara Small.

I thank each of you for the many hours you have spent reading these chapters, for bringing plot inconsistencies and errors to my attention, and for your endless encouragement.

I also want to thank Curtis West and Michael Johnson for sharing their expertise in the construction field.

Thank you, dear friends.

Chapter 1

It was drizzling the day they arrived in Paris. Charles held the umbrella, and Sarah gripped his arm, snuggling against him as they walked. "I'm glad we waited until now," she said, looking up at her husband of four months with a twinkle in her eye.

Charles wrapped his arm around her and pulled her even closer. "I'm just glad we're finally here." They'd been planning their honeymoon for several months but had decided to wait for warm weather. They were married during one of the worst snowstorms the Midwest had seen for years and decided it was no time to be at the mercy of the airlines.

It was early spring and, despite the light rain, Sarah found Paris to be breathtaking.

Earlier that day, they had taken a cab from the airport to their hotel in Montmartre. The driver offered to give them a quick sightseeing tour through the downtown area and past the Louvre; along the way, he pointed out popular shops, the museums, and bridges crossing the Seine to the Left Bank.

Their hotel was situated above the city, halfway up the hill leading to the Sacré-Coeur. From their fifth-floor window, Sarah could look out over the rooftops of the city. "What an awesome view," she exclaimed when Charles joined her at the window. Their room was spacious and comfortably decorated, although they knew they probably wouldn't spend much time there considering all the sightseeing they had planned.

Sarah picked up a brochure that described several nearby restaurants and cafés, along with a list of things to do in Paris and a street map. But after scanning the brochure, she realized that ten days might not be enough time to see all the things they hoped to see.

After getting settled and freshened up, they left the hotel on foot. Glancing down at the map she was carrying, Sarah commented, "Paris is much smaller than I realized. I think we can walk to most things."

"It's not quite that small, but we can use the metro and cabs," he responded. "How about grabbing some lunch?" Charles asked cheerfully as he picked up the pace.

"Hey! I'm taking three steps for every one of yours," she teased. "Slow down!"

"Sorry," he responded, pulling her close and attempting to adapt to her pace.

"And," she added, "I don't think one *grabs lunch* in Paris. I believe the French have developed the art of savoring their meals."

They stopped at a café up the street from their hotel and were led to a small round table near the window. Charles reached across the table and took her hand. "Are you happy?"

"Ecstatic!" Sarah giggled with the excitement of a child at a theme park. "But I'm trying to act my age," she added, attempting to present a demeanor more in keeping with her years. *Seventy years old and a blushing bride*, she thought. Her face became flushed at the thought.

It had been twenty years since her husband, Jonathan, had died, and she had become accustomed to her life as a widow. A few years ago, she had retired and moved to a retirement community, Cunningham Village, where she made friends, learned to quilt, and was enjoying her independence. And then she met Charles.

Charles was a detective, retired from the local police department. A serious stroke brought him to Cunningham Village, where he spent many months in their rehab center before settling into one of their apartments that offered assisted living. He no longer needed special services and was totally independent when he met Sarah, but he had decided to continue living in the community. He fell in love with Sarah the day they met.

In fact, Charles would tell you he fell in love with her long before that. He was the police officer who notified Sarah that her husband had suffered a fatal accident on the job. Charles never forgot this lovely, gentle woman, but she had been too grief-stricken to be aware of him back then.

"Look!" Sarah exclaimed, pointing toward the sky. "It's stopped raining, and I think the sun's coming out."

"What would you like to do today?" Charles asked as the waitress was serving their drinks.

"I'd like to walk. I want to get to know Paris, and there's no better way! Let's start with the Sacré-Coeur." Handing him the map she added, "It's only a short walk from here, and it overlooks the city."

"It's a short walk, *all uphill*," Charles responded with a chuckle.

"But then it's *downhill* coming back," she replied with a reassuring twinkle in her eye.

The young waitress arrived with their lunches and refilled their wine glasses from the decanter of chardonnay that had been placed between them. Charles had ordered Provençal slow-roasted pork and *pommes frites*, which he later learned was a very fancy way of saying french fries. Sarah, wanting to experience something new, ordered a goat cheese salad served with raspberry honey dressing and a French baguette. "No escargot?" Charles asked teasingly.

"Not yet, but I'll get there before the week is over." The couple enjoyed a relaxed meal, savoring the food and enjoying the atmosphere.

"Are you ready to climb the hill?" she asked as they left the café.

"Ready and able," he responded, pulling the map out of his breast pocket. "I think we should head up past that cemetery and pick up Rue de la Bonne. It looks like that street goes right up to the Basilica." As they walked along the cobblestone sidewalk, signs confirmed that they had chosen well. Suddenly the narrow cobblestone road took a left turn and opened up at the foot of the Sacré-Coeur Basilica, which loomed high above them.

"Magnificent!" Sarah gasped, not prepared for the splendor of the architecture. As they climbed the multitude of steps up to the portico, they both became very quiet, respecting the sacredness of their surroundings. Once inside, they sat in the opulent sanctuary and held hands without speaking. Sarah had tears in her eyes as they walked to the marble steps leading up to the dome.

Looking out over Paris, Sarah revised her earlier statement. "I guess it's not as small as I thought it was," she said, gazing over the mass of rooftops spreading out in all directions. "Is that the Seine I see over there, just beyond the Eiffel Tower?" she asked, pointing toward what appeared to be water snaking through the city.

"Yes, and I want to spend our last night in Paris drifting down the Seine on a romantic dinner cruise," Charles said, pulling her close to him.

Sarah nodded enthusiastically adding, "And I want to walk across the bridges in the rain like they do in the movies!"

Charles laughed. "And I'll sing and dance with a cane and a top hat!"

By the time they returned to their hotel room, neither was interested in walking over a bridge or anywhere else. Their feet hurt from their new shoes, and Charles' arthritis in his right hip was causing him discomfort. They had dinner sent up to their room, and they stretched out on the bed watching *The Expendables*, with Arnold Schwarzenegger speaking French. Charles seemed to be enjoying it. As Sarah turned over and closed her eyes, she muttered, "You owe me one *chick flick*."

Before they knew it, they were on the plane flying home, leaving Paris and their many adventures far behind them. They couldn't believe how fast the days flew by. They were sad to see their honeymoon end, but they were both eager to return to their new life as *Mr. and Mrs. Parker*.

Had they known what was in store for them, they wouldn't have been so eager.

Chapter 2

"I have a question." Sophie was sitting on her front porch, shelling walnuts for a baklava recipe she was determined to try.

"What's your question?" Sarah asked, looking up from the colorful little quilt she was hemming for her granddaughter, Alaina.

Sophie avoided her eyes and seemed to be hesitant to ask her question.

"Well …?" Sarah said with raised eyebrows. "What do you want to ask me?"

"Okay. Here goes. What's going on across the street? I see you and Charles there for a week or so; then you're both gone. Then one day I see you there, and I don't see Charles for several days. Are you two living there or at his apartment? I thought the plan was for Charles to move in with you once you were married. Is there a problem of some kind?"

"No, Sophie, there really isn't a problem. Well, at least nothing we can't resolve." Sarah hesitantly added, "It's just that …"

Sophie held her hand up to stop Sarah mid-sentence. "Stop. This is none of my business, Sarah. I shouldn't have asked. You don't need to answer."

Sarah laid her sewing aside and moved her chair closer to Sophie. "I'm sorry I haven't talked to you about this before. I've been trying to figure it out myself. I guess I just didn't know where to start."

Looking worried, Sophie said, "This sounds serious."

"It's not really that, Sophie. It's just … how can I explain it? It's just that Charles and I have both lived alone for so many years, and we've developed our own ways of doing things. They're little things, but we're getting on each other's nerves. If we were young, there would be nothing to it. We'd just compromise and change. But you know how it is with older folks …"

"Set in our ways!" Sophie exclaimed, nodding. "But you two can work this out, can't you?" she asked, still looking worried about her friends. "Maybe these houses are just too small for a couple."

"That's exactly what I thought the problem was until we went to Paris. But while we were there, we lived in one room and did just fine. We finally realized what it was. Everything there was *ours*. Not his. Not mine. But *ours*. We weren't on my turf or his turf. We were in a place we shared."

"So that's the answer! Move to a place that belongs to both of you. Simple," Sophie said, with a hand gesture that indicated the problem was solved.

"We thought that was the answer, but that's when we ran into the bigger problem. Where is that shared place going to be? I want to stay right here in Cunningham Village. This has become my home, and a retirement community is perfect for us for the rest of our lives. And besides that, I have family and friends here, and you're like a sister to me."

Sophie smiled, unable to admit she felt the same way about Sarah but very touched to hear Sarah say it. "You're my buddy!" she responded and turned away to avoid eye contact. Expressing feelings was not Sophie's forte.

"So what's the problem?" Sophie asked. "He's happy here, too, isn't he? Just buy one of those lots up on the knoll and build a house that's just right for both of you. That's going to be part of Cunningham Village when it's finished, and you'll have the benefit of everything the Village has to offer."

"We've talked about that, but he has another idea. He'd like for us to move to Colorado to be near his sons. They've had a tumultuous relationship over the years. Charles was a good cop, but I wonder if he was able to make time for the family. His boys seem to be very bitter."

"Didn't his wife die while the boys were still at home?"

"Yes. She was sick for a number of years and died when the boys were in their early teens. He admits he threw himself into his job and was home even less after that. I guess they blamed him—or resented him. You know how kids can be. Anyway, he seems to think he can make it up to them by being around now."

"That's not going to happen," Sophie responded emphatically.

"I know, but he wants to try."

"So he wants the two of you to move to Colorado?"

"Yes."

"But your kids …?"

"I know."

"I see the problem."

The two women sat quietly for a while, each lost in her own thoughts. Finally, Sophie shrugged and resumed cracking walnut shells. Sarah picked up her needle but didn't begin sewing right away. "We'll make it through this, Sophie. I know we will. We care very deeply for one another, and I'm sure we can find common ground. It'll just take time." She picked up her granddaughter's little quilt and resumed attaching the binding with tiny hem stitches. *I can't leave my family and live several thousand miles away*, she told herself silently.

* * * * *

"We're going to drive up to the waterfall today for our first picnic of the spring," Jason announced when Sarah answered the phone.

"It's a perfect day for it," Sarah responded with a smile.

"Well?"

"Well, what?" she asked.

"Well, what's your answer? Will you and Charles go with us?"

Sarah laughed, recognizing that Jason always started in the middle of the conversation as if she had been there for the thoughts he had before he spoke. Jason was her forty-one-year-old son and the father of her only grandchild. Little Alaina was six months old and adorable. She was an easygoing child who giggled easily and seemed to love everyone she met.

"We'd love to go. Did you invite Martha?"

"I called her, but she wasn't home. I left a message, and I hope she'll be able to go. I haven't seen much of my sister lately."

"She's probably at the lab."

"It's Saturday!" he exploded. "Doesn't that woman know how to relax?"

"She's learning, now that you mention it. You know, she had a few dates with Sophie's son when he was in town. Actually, more than a few," she corrected herself, "and she told me last week that she's considering a trip to Alaska to see him!"

"Wow! That doesn't sound like my work-obsessed sister."

"I think she's smitten," Sarah responded, smiling. "So what time are you going on this picnic, and what can I bring?"

"I'm bringing a box of hamburgers and the makings for a fire. I was hoping Charles would cook for us. He's great with the grill. And I'll put Jenny on the phone to talk to you about the other details. Jenny …" he yelled. "Come talk to Mom."

"Hi, Mom," Jenny said as she picked up the phone. Sarah could hear Alaina in the background making those endearing noises that babies make. "Are you going to join us?" she asked.

"Absolutely. Charles went out for a haircut, but I know he'll be excited about it. So what can I bring?"

"I think we have it covered. I made a bowl of potato salad. We have rolls and the fixings for the burgers. I have lots of chips and dip stuff, and I might bring some fruit. Maybe Charles could pick up some beer? We have sodas in the cooler already. Oh, I know! Do you have paper plates?"

"A whole shelf full. I'll bring all the paper goods and plastic cups. Also, I made a chocolate cake with raspberry filling yesterday. We still have most of it. I'll bring that, too."

"Sounds perfect. It's been a cold winter, and it'll be great to get out in the spring sunshine. It's going to be in the low eighties today!" she said enthusiastically. "A perfect day for a picnic!" Sarah loved Jennifer's ability to appreciate the small things in life. "Shall we pick you up?" Jenny added.

"No. We'll meet you there." They agreed to meet in the early afternoon at the bottom of the waterfall. Sarah decided to ask Charles about going a little early so they could grab a prime location and start the fire.

After she hung up, Sarah dialed Martha's cell phone and, sure enough, she was at work. She told her about the picnic and could hear her daughter's hesitation. "I really should finish …"

"Martha! It's Saturday. Do you have a deadline?"

"No, not really. I just wanted to get a head start on this project," she said, but then she laughed and added, "but a picnic sounds much better. Do I have time to run home and change?"

"Absolutely. Charles and I will pick you up around noon, okay?"

As she opened the pantry and began pulling out the paper goods left from the previous summer, she realized she was humming. "Life is good," she said aloud to herself.

"What about the kids?" Charles asked as they were packing up the car later that morning. He was referring to their dog, Barney, and Barney's kitten, Boots. They had called her Bootsy when Barney found her. She was tiny, helpless, and nearly frozen when Barney heard her crying from inside a snow-covered bush at the dog park. But now, five months later, she was a beautiful young cat who pranced around proudly in her snow-white fur boots.

Barney could tell something was up, and his tail wagged happily as he ran around in circles. "Barney can go," Sarah called from the backyard, "but, of course, Boots will be staying home." Barney was getting used to the idea of leaving his kitten home. She slept in her *grown-up* bed now but still snuck into Barney's basket occasionally and curled up against his safe, warm body. She had been much too young to be away from her mother when they found her, and she occasionally required some nurturing, which Barney was happy to provide.

As the three piled into the car and headed for Martha's house, Sarah looked at Charles and smiled. He reached over and patted her leg and winked. At that moment, she knew they would find a solution to their dilemma. She knew they loved each other enough to make whatever compromises were necessary to make their marriage work. She winked back at this wonderful man who had brought romance into her life when she least expected it.

Chapter 3

Sarah was trembling as she took her place at the front of the small classroom in the back of Ruth's quilt shop. Sarah had only been quilting for a couple of years and was surprised when Ruth, the owner of Running Stitches, asked her to teach beginning quilting. Ruth had confidence in her ability and had reassured her over and over that she could do it. Sarah had developed her own class itinerary and was comfortable with what she would be teaching. *Why am I so nervous?* she asked herself.

There were five women signed up for the class, and three were already there. Sarah hoped the other two were coming soon since she was eager to get started. While they waited, she decided to pass the time with introductions.

"Hello, everyone. I'm Sarah Miller, and this class is Introduction to Quilting. This is a beginning class, and we'll be exploring the basics of machine piecing. The only prerequisite is that you know how to use a sewing machine. You're going to learn enough to make a simple throw, like the one I have hanging here." Sarah pointed to the sample quilt she had made for the class. She had chosen a simple pattern that featured six-inch blocks of focus fabric alternating with

Four-Patch blocks of coordinating fabrics. "As you can see, I've used one fabric for the square and two fabrics for the four-patches. There are also two borders: one narrow and one about four inches wide." Noticing that two of the students were taking notes, she added, "I'll be passing out instructions, and we'll go over all of this later. I just wanted you to see the finished product so you could start thinking about what colors you want to use for your quilts.

"What I'd like to do next is hear from you. Please tell us your name, your sewing experience, and why you decided to take this class."

"Let's start here," Sarah said, stopping in front of a slim young woman dressed in jeans, a white tunic, and a short denim vest. Sarah smiled, noticing that the young woman appeared nervous too. She hoped her own uneasiness wasn't as apparent as this young woman's was.

"Hi. I'm Brenda Lee. I'm married and have two toddlers, both boys. I'm here to get out of the house," she said with a nervous giggle, and everyone laughed. "No, really—I want to learn to quilt, but getting a break from a couple of wild youngsters is a real benefit." The other women in the class chuckled, nodded their heads in agreement, and offered words of encouragement. Brenda Lee looked around, and Sarah saw her shoulders relax as a grateful smile crossed her face.

"Oh!" she added, remembering there was another part to the question. "I took sewing in high school. I'll admit I haven't used it much over the last ten years, but I made my own clothes back then."

"Thank you, Brenda Lee. Who wants to go next?"

"I'm Doris," the woman sitting next to Brenda Lee announced. "I've been sewing all my life, and that's a long, *long* time!" she said, laughing, and the group laughed with her. Doris was in her sixties and went on to explain that, over the years, she had made her own curtains and drapes and had even reupholstered her couch the previous year. "Now I need a quilt to put on the back of that couch," she added, half joking. "The truth is I've always wanted to quilt but never really enjoyed handwork. When I realized that quilts could be made on the machine, I decided to give it a try."

"You're in the right place for that, Doris. And you'll leave this class with a quilt for that couch!"

The third person was a frail-looking woman who had chosen a seat in the back of the classroom. Looking toward her, Sarah said, "Wouldn't you like to move up here with us?"

The woman nodded, stood, and walked slowly to the front of the room. Sarah noticed she was limping and had left her cane in the back of the room. She appeared to be in pain. The woman sat down gingerly at the table next to Doris.

"So, tell us about yourself. What's your name?" Sarah said as she walked to the back of the room and moved the woman's cane up to her new seat.

"Thank you," the woman said to Sarah. Then turning to the others, she said, "I'm Myrtle. I made all my kid's clothes when they were young. I even made clothes for my grandchildren, but now I'm a great-grandma. I want to make things for the kids, but youngsters these days don't like the kinds of clothes I make. You know what I mean? I can't make the odd stuff kids wear now, and actually I wouldn't want to," she added. "Anyway, I was thinking maybe I could make quilts for them. Kids still like that kind of thing, don't they?"

"Absolutely, Myrtle. Kids love quilts, and there are wonderful children's fabrics to choose from. How old are your grandchildren?"

"Well … let me see. Tyrone is twelve now. Anika is ten. The little ones are three and five. My granddaughter's got her hands full, that's for sure," she added, shaking her head.

"I think they'll love getting quilts from their great-grandma!" Sarah assured her.

"Okay. We have two other people who signed up for the class. We'll have to catch them up later. I'll tell you a little about myself. As I said earlier, my name is Sarah Miller."

Sarah paused, and then looked embarrassed. "Wait! That's not my name! I got married on New Year's Eve and …" Everyone clapped and congratulated her.

"Let me start over. My name is Sarah *Parker*! But call me Sarah." She had decided not to tell the class that she had only been quilting for a couple of years. She had a good grasp on the basic skills, and she figured there was no reason to cause her students to doubt her ability.

"As I said earlier, we'll be making this quilt," she said, pointing again to the hanging quilt. "You'll be learning how to choose your fabrics, how to read and follow the pattern, how to cut accurately, how to sew a precise quarter-inch seam, and how to square up your finished blocks. Then we'll be putting rows together and adding borders. After that, we'll choose fabric for the back and make the binding. At that point, it'll be ready to quilt."

Sarah had left one section of the binding open on her sample quilt so she could show the class the parts of a quilt and how they got quilted together to form the final quilt.

"Will we be quilting ours as well?"

"That's up to you. I can show you how to do simple straight-line quilting. If you want to wait, Ruth will offer a machine quilting class later in the year. Alternatively, I send mine to a longarm machine quilter and pay to have it finished. And, of course, you can always hand quilt it if you want. We can refer you to a woman who teaches hand quilting and another who will hand quilt it for you if anyone's interested."

After a few other questions, Sarah passed out the pattern and the supply list. As they read through the pattern, the class had questions about making the four-patches, but Sarah assured them that they would learn that when the time came. "Right now," she said, "let's concentrate on the fabric." She pointed out the fabric requirements on the pattern.

The rest of the afternoon was spent in the shop, putting compatible bolts together and learning about small, medium, and large patterns and light, medium, and dark fabrics. Sarah talked about value and hue, but ultimately, seeing her student's eyes beginning to haze over, she said, "Put together what looks good to you and then bring it over here. I'll take a look and make suggestions if you want me to."

By the end of the class, everyone was lined up at the cash register with their fabrics and any supplies they didn't already have. All three needed cutting boards, twenty-four–inch rulers, rotary cutters, and thread.

After everyone had left, Sarah collapsed in one of the classroom chairs with a cup of coffee. "How did it go?" Ruth asked.

"Once I figured out what my name was, it went fine," she said shaking her head. "I must have been even more nervous than I thought I was. Anyway, it went fine, but I only had three students. The other two didn't show up."

"Oh. I forgot to tell you. The Manahan sisters called to cancel. Their mother had a heart attack and is in ICU. They're flying down to Florida to be with her. I'll refund their deposit, and they can take your next class."

"My next class?" Sarah said, looking over at Ruth inquisitively.

"Yes, I'm putting your name on the website as our Introduction to Quilting teacher. Okay?"

Sarah smiled her acceptance but looked away, thinking about Charles' desire to move to Colorado.

Chapter 4

"Hi, sweetie. I'm glad you got home early. I was wondering if you'd like to go out to dinner tonight to celebrate."

"I would love to go out, but what are we celebrating?"

"Well, it's May first ..." Charles responded somewhat mysteriously.

"And we're celebrating May Day?"

"We can do that while we're out, but I was thinking about our anniversary."

"Our anniversary?"

"Yes! Today is our four-month anniversary. We've been married exactly one-third of a year!"

Sarah laughed. "Of course I would love to go out with you and celebrate, but if we're celebrating our anniversary, why don't we walk over to the Community Center and have dinner in the restaurant where we got married?"

"Great idea," he responded, looking at her with tenderness. "You were so beautiful walking down the aisle on Jason's arm."

"You weren't so bad yourself in your black tux and your lavender satin cummerbund ..."

"… to match your flowers and Sophie's dress. By the way," he added, looking puzzled, "why did I have to match Sophie's dress?"

"Your cummerbund wasn't lavender in order to match Sophie's dress, you silly man. It was lavender because our colors were antique white and lavender. Remember my dress?"

"Vividly! It was this creamy-colored long thing, sort of shiny in places when you moved. And I think your arms sort of peeked out somehow …"

"I'm glad you weren't writing the wedding announcement for the newspaper. 'The bride wore a shiny long thing …'"

"Your dress was spectacular, my dear. You were the most beautiful bride there ever was."

Sarah pictured herself lined up with all the twenty-something young women that probably got married that same night. At seventy, she was definitely *not* the most beautiful bride, but she wasn't going to argue if that's how Charles remembered it.

In fact, her dress was a very pale cream color; the label described it as antique white. It was satin and had a short channel-type bolero with sleeves of handmade lace. When Sarah saw the dress in the shop, she thought she recognized it and hurried home to pull out an old photograph album. Sure enough, it was a near replica of the dress her mother had worn. Sarah's grandmother had made that dress by hand for her daughter's wedding, which had been scheduled for June 1943 but was delayed until the war ended. They were married in the winter of 1945.

Sarah hadn't wanted to pay that much for her dress. She had been picturing something much less formal since they were planning a simple wedding at the Community Center. But when she saw the dress, she knew it was perfect. Her mother would have loved it. It surprised her at the time that, despite her age, she still wished her mother could have been there.

"Has your mind wandered?" Charles asked. She hadn't said much since they arrived at the Community Center restaurant.

"I was picturing this room the way it was that night with all our friends here."

"It was a New Year's Eve party I'll never forget!" he responded, taking her hand across the table as they reminisced.

The party had started off with hors d'oeuvres and dancing, followed by an elegant catered dinner. Sophie had arranged for the band that played at her son's welcome home party the previous fall.

Most of Sarah's friends were there, including Ruth and Anna from the quilt shop; Andy and his daughter, Caitlyn; and many of her neighbors and quilting friends. And, of course, her family: Jason and Jennifer with little Alaina, sleeping in her carry-along sleeper, and Martha gently rocking it with her foot.

Charles had invited a few of his old friends from the police department and Graham Holtz, his attorney and life-long friend who had been at his first wedding. Charles also invited Percy and Dell, who were two elderly men he played cards with.

Sarah's only regret was that Charles' sons hadn't made the effort to come. They both said they were busy at work and couldn't get away. Sarah had hoped to meet them and had written them individually to invite them. They responded by telephone to Charles, saying they wouldn't be coming. She knew he was hurt.

The waiter interrupted their thoughts suddenly when he brought their meals. Charles had ordered for them and, to her surprise, had ordered the exact dinner that was served the night of their wedding. They drank a toast to their many years ahead, neither wanting to bring up the subject of where those years would be spent. After dinner, they walked home holding hands under the stars. It was a cool spring evening, and as they walked, they continued to think about the night they were married.

Sophie and Sarah had requested a vacant room where they could change for the late-night ceremony. While they were dressing, the staff rearranged the main room, making rows of seating for the guests and an aisle for the bridal party. All the flowers were moved to the front of the room, and the minister took his place. When Sarah peeked into the room, expecting to see the banquet room from earlier, she saw instead a wedding chapel. The band began to play the Wedding March.

Sophie had turned to Sarah, saying, "Why are they starting so early? This was supposed to be a New Year's wedding, and it's not even midnight yet."

"Just wait," Sarah responded. "You'll see."

Sophie, as Sarah's matron of honor, walked down the aisle in her lavender dress and long jacket. She carried her new rhinestone-studded cane. Her friend, Andy, led her slowly down the aisle.

Sarah and her handsome son, Jason, were next. As they walked down the aisle, Sarah smiled at her friends as they turned to admire the elegant bride.

Right behind them was their special ring bearer, Barney, with a purple ribbon around his neck that held the wedding bands.

As Sarah took her place next to Charles, she heard Sophie grumbling, "It's still not midnight!"

"Just wait," Sarah whispered.

The minister said his piece and instructed the couple to join hands. They had written their own vows, but Charles was too emotional to remember his. He simply looked at his bride apologetically and said, "I love you ..."

She responded softly with a loving smile. "Me, too."

They exchanged rings, the minister hesitated for a few seconds, looked at his watch, and finally said, "I now pronounce you man and wife ... and Happy New Year!"

Confetti flew, balloons dropped from the ceiling, and the band played Auld Lang Syne.

It was a night to remember.

Chapter 5

Sarah arrived early for her class the next week and was surprised to see two of her students already in the shop. Sarah had been thinking about a new line of fabric that had been nagging at her creative side. "I want to take a serious look at that oriental fabric line," she told Anna, who was covering the shop while Ruth finished teaching her morning class. "It's not like anything I've worked with before, but it just intrigues me!"

Sarah headed for the shelf of Asian-inspired fabrics and pulled down the first bolt that caught her eye. The fabric had a black background and featured beautifully dressed women wearing intricate kimonos and sitting gracefully in a parklike setting. They were surrounded by an array of flowers including peonies, wisteria, dahlias, and plum flowers in pinks, yellows, and lavenders. Branches of cherry blossoms hung delicately above their heads.

"The geisha are beautiful in that fabric, aren't they?" Anna said.

"Geisha? But I thought …" Sarah said hesitantly, looking somewhat embarrassed.

A customer standing nearby spoke up. "You thought they were *ladies of the night*, didn't you?" she chuckled. "That's a common misconception." The woman speaking had a thick British accent. "I'm so sorry to be caught listening to your conversation," she said, looking contrite.

"I'm glad you spoke up," Sarah responded, introducing herself and Anna. "I'd love to hear more about these exotic-looking women."

"I'm Amelia. I'm glad to meet you both, and again, please forgive my rude behavior. I shouldn't have interrupted, but I couldn't resist. My husband and I lived in Japan for many years, and I thought the same thing when we first arrived. But I learned that geisha are very talented women who are rigorously trained for years in the traditional Japanese art of song, dance, communication, and hospitality. They entertain in the finest teahouses and have been a part of Japanese culture for over 400 years. Their intricate kimonos, their white makeup, their elaborate hairdos are all works of art." Amelia went on to tell them details about the geisha way of life. "They are highly respected in Japanese culture."

Sarah and Anna were fascinated by Amelia's stories. As they talked, Sarah looked again at the women on the beautiful fabrics. "I don't know where I got the idea that they were disreputable."

"I do," the woman said, smiling. "During the war, there were young Japanese women who imitated the geisha manner of dress and made money selling themselves to the soldiers. They were called *geisha girls*. They were poor imitations of the real thing."

The women continued to talk for a while, and Sarah looked at the Asian fabrics with a new eye as the woman told them stories from her years spent in Japan.

Later, Anna followed the woman to the cash register, where she rang up the book the woman was purchasing about traditional American quilts. "I don't quilt, but I'm interested in learning someday." Anna told her about Sarah's class, and Amelia turned to wave at Sarah as she left the shop. "I just might be seeing you next fall," she called to Sarah as she left the store.

Returning to the fabric aisle, Anna asked Sarah if she were interested in making an Asian-inspired quilt.

"Yes, but I have no idea what kind of pattern I would use. I wouldn't want to cut this piece up," she said, pointing to the geisha fabric, "but I really love it."

"That piece is a panel, Sarah, and is usually used as a center with borders or other blocks around it. We have several new books with patterns for Asian-inspired quilts if you would like to look at them. We haven't even put them out yet."

While Anna walked to the back room to get the books, Sarah pulled several other bolts from the shelf and lined them on the table Ruth provided for her customers. Some of the bolts featured flowers alone, while others were interspersed with cranes, butterflies, and pagodas. By the time Anna returned with the books, Sarah had a dozen bolts of fabric lined up on the table.

"I wonder if I could fussy cut the geisha out of the panel and use them with some of these other fabrics?"

"Take a look at this pattern," Anna said, pointing to the quilt on the cover of one of the books. "This is similar to what you're describing."

"Yes! That's exactly what I'm picturing, but it looks very complicated."

Anna opened the book and skimmed through the instructions. "I don't think you'd have any trouble with this, Sarah. It looks complicated, but it's primarily four-patches and half-square triangles. You can do this easily."

Sarah continued to run her hands over the fabrics. She sighed and said, "These fabrics touch me. There is something exciting about them. Something mysterious and exciting."

"I agree. Would you like to take this book? You could look at the other quilts and decide if you want to make one."

"I want to take the book, but I don't need to decide. I already know that I want to make this one," she responded, pointing to the quilt Anna had shown her. "How much fabric will I need?"

Turning to the directions, Anna responded, "The pattern calls for ten different fabrics including the borders. Let's see what we can put together."

The two women examined the bolts Sarah had placed on the table and added two more from the shelf. "What do you think?" Anna asked.

"I was hoping to use parts of the panel. None of these has geisha."

"Okay. Let's look at the pattern again," Anna said, turning to a page with details about the layout. "How about you cut the geisha out of the panel and use them in these six-inch squares where they have the focus fabric?"

"I love it," Sarah said enthusiastically. "That's perfect!" Sarah placed the panel on the table and removed her least favorite, allowing the panel to take its place. They decided which pieces would be the borders, and Anna put a sticky note on each bolt indicating the amount she would need to cut.

"Okay—we're ready to cut," Anna said, and the two women carried the bolts to the cutting table.

As Anna was cutting the panel, Sarah said, "Instead of two panels, I think I'll take three since I might lose a few of the geisha when I'm fussy cutting."

Charles had teased her about fussy cutting. He had asked her what the term meant, and when she showed him how she would carefully cut around a design she wanted to feature, he started using the term copiously. In fact, when he served her a piece of birthday cake, he cut a round piece out of the middle of the cake, carefully cutting around the rose adornment and announced that it had been *fussy cut* just for her.

By the time her students began to arrive for the afternoon class, Sarah had a bag of fabric, a book, and an excited expression on her face. "What's going on?" Ruth asked Sarah as she was entering the classroom. Sarah told her about her plans, and as her students arrived, she was persuaded to take the fabric out and tell them about her project.

As the students were taking their places at the machines, Ruth came back in and introduced a young man named Christopher. While he was getting acquainted with the other students, Ruth took a fourth machine out of the cupboard and set it up on the table next to Myrtle.

"Just call me Chris," he was telling the other students. Chris was in his mid-thirties and said he recently lost his job, and he wanted to spend some of his free time using the sewing machine and fabric his mother had left.

They later learned that his mother had died several years ago, and her quilting supplies had been packed up and stored in the attic. Chris had been living there with a girlfriend but was alone now. "She wasn't interested in a relationship with an unemployed store clerk," he had said with an embarrassed chuckle.

He told Sarah that his mother had been a gifted quilter, and he would like to learn the skill. "I think she would have liked that," he said wistfully.

Chris had grown up watching his mother sew, and he knew many of the basics. Ruth helped him choose his fabrics, and he caught up with the class quickly.

The second class focused on cutting out fabric. Sarah went over the cutting instructions first; then she demonstrated using the rotary cutter. Although Sarah emphasized the importance of keeping the rotary cutter closed when not in use, Brenda Lee laid hers on the cutting mat still open and when she reached for it, she cut her finger. "My fabric is ruined," she wailed as the blood dripped on the fabric she was preparing to cut.

"It's just on the corner, Brenda Lee. We can cut that part off."

Doris had Band-Aids in her sewing basket and came to Brenda Lee's aid. Once things had settled down again and the students began to cut, Myrtle's ruler slipped when she was making a long cut, resulting in her two-inch strip now being two inches wide at one end and one and a half inches on the other. Sarah took the ruined piece out to Ruth and asked her to cut another strip from the bolt. While she was in the shop, she grabbed a package of rubber circles that could be attached to the back of the ruler to keep it from skidding. Everyone in the class decided to put them on their rulers as well.

Chris was the only one who could handle the rotary cutter proficiently, and he ended up helping Myrtle, who continued to have problems.

"If you have trouble with the other quilts you plan to make at home," Sarah said to her after class, "come in and we'll help you cut it out."

Everyone finished cutting and had their fabric labeled and ready to begin sewing the next week. As they were getting ready to leave, Doris asked if they could sew their strips at home.

"No, Doris. Today we looked at the importance of precise, careful cutting, and next week we'll be looking at the importance of the quarter-inch seam allowance. I'll show you some techniques for ensuring that your seam is accurate. Then we'll do our sewing together, and if we have time, we'll make our four-patches."

Doris, who was more experienced than the other students, decided she wanted to make a second quilt at home using the same pattern. "I need a gift for my daughter's birthday, and this would be a terrific surprise for her. She doesn't know I'm taking this class."

Sarah was pleased that Doris was taking her experience beyond the class project. "I think that's a fantastic idea, Doris. If you need any help choosing the fabrics, Ruth is out in the shop and will be happy to help you."

As they were leaving the classroom, Sarah noticed that Myrtle was having trouble getting up from her chair, and she hurried over to give her a hand. "I'm sorry," Myrtle muttered. "This ol' hip of mine is really acting up. The doc wants to give me a new one, and I guess I should do it. It really scares me, though," she added, shaking her head. "I just don't know."

"Is someone picking you up, or did you drive here?" Sarah asked.

"Oh, I just live a couple of blocks up the street. I walked over. The exercise is good for me."

"How about I drive you today, Myrtle? They're predicting rain tonight, and if you're anything like me, the old joints can really complain when the weather changes."

"That's for sure!" Myrtle responded with a knowing grin. "But you're a long way from old, Mrs. Parker."

"Call me Sarah, and I just had my seventieth birthday."

"See? You're a youngster. I'll be turning eighty next week."

"We're both youngsters," Sarah laughed. "Let me drive you today, okay?"

"I'd be much appreciative," Myrtle responded, leaving the room while leaning heavily on her cane. "I need thread, so I'll go get that while you're packing up. Don't hurry."

Eighty years old and taking a class to learn something new! Sarah had tremendous respect for this woman who didn't let her age or her pain keep her from life. She made a mental note to bring a cake to the next class so the group could celebrate Myrtle's birthday.

"What an adorable house," Sarah commented as she pulled up to the curb where Myrtle had indicated. It was a small brick house with red shutters. A pink dogwood to the left of the walkway was in bloom, and a short picket fence enclosed a yard that was filled with spring flowers. "Do you do your own gardening?"

"I found a young man to help me this year. Edward took care of it until he died last fall." She looked away, avoiding Sarah's eyes.

"Your husband?"

"Yes."

"I'm sorry."

Realizing Myrtle didn't want to talk about it, she quickly changed the subject. "I'm excited about the quilts you're planning for your great-grandchildren. The one you are working on in class is adorable." Myrtle had chosen brown and green fabrics with an animal motif, which she said the middle boy would love.

"I hope you'll bring the other quilts in to show us when you finish them."

"Lord willing," she responded as she shuffled up the walkway toward her door. Sarah waited until she was inside before driving away. *So many people carry sadness that they hide from the world.*

Sarah made the decision to have a serious talk with Charles about their future. "We're not youngsters," she had told Sophie the previous day. "How many years can we possibly have together? We shouldn't waste a single day arguing about where to live."

"Would you move?" Sophie had asked.

"If necessary," she had responded, "but I hope it won't come to that." *Lord willing.*

Chapter 6

"Good morning, my love." Charles had just come out of the bedroom, and as usual, he was cheerful, freshly showered, and fully dressed for the day. Sarah loved that about him. She was still in her dressing gown but only because she was letting him use their only facilities. "We need two bathrooms," he said as if he read her thoughts.

"Absolutely. We need two bathrooms and a larger house to wrap around them." She poured their coffee, slipped freshly baked biscuits out of the oven, and served them along with a bowl of eggs scrambled with onions and mushrooms.

"That's what smelled so good!" Charles exclaimed as she set the food on the table.

After they ate and she had poured their second cup of coffee, she looked at him seriously and said, "Charles, we need to talk."

"That sounds ominous," he said, looking guilty. "What did I do wrong?"

Despite the seriousness of the subject, Sarah couldn't help but laugh at his response. "You're such a little boy! You didn't do a thing wrong. We just need to decide what we're going to do about a home of our own."

Looking contrite, he responded, "I know, and I'm sorry to make light of it. We can't keep putting this off. I've been thinking about this idea of mine that we move to Colorado."

"And …?"

"I'm beginning to think it might be a bad idea," he announced, much to Sarah's surprise. "I look at you and your family, and I know it wouldn't be right for you to be so far from them. And it probably wouldn't solve my problem anyway. So I think we should give up on the idea of moving out there."

Sarah sighed with relief. "Thank you, Charles. Thank you for understanding that."

"But," he continued, "I still want to build a relationship with my boys."

"What do you have in mind?"

"I was hoping that you and I could visit them once or twice a year, and maybe, off in the future, they'd be willing to come here for a visit."

"Also phone calls in the interim," Sarah suggested. "And even emails?"

"Yes. So how about we go out there for a few weeks? It would give us a chance to spend time with them, and it would be a little vacation for us. What do you think?"

Sarah hesitated for a moment and then replied, "I'd need to think about this, Charles, but my immediate thought is that this first trip is something you should do alone. I think adding me to the equation just gives the boys another issue between you and them. I don't think they're comfortable with our marriage. They hardly acknowledged our wedding. I think you need to spend time with them by yourself first and see what you can do about reconnecting with them."

Charles looked down at his coffee cup and nodded his head. "I'm afraid you're right. I'd miss you, but this is probably something I should do alone." He sighed and gently pushed his coffee cup away. "I'll think about it and maybe call John and sound him out about a visit."

"Will you call David?"

"I'll call John first, but then I'll see if David will talk to me."

Sarah knew how important it was to Charles that he connected with his sons, but she felt it was going to be an uphill battle. He and his boys had never been *a family*. During their mother's long illness, her sister, Sylvia, had provided much of the boys' care. Charles worked long hours and was rarely home.

After their mother's death, the boys moved in with Sylvia. The year they graduated from high school, their Aunt Sylvia and her husband moved to Denver, and Charles agreed to let them take the boys. "I couldn't take care of them," he had told Sarah. "I was emotionally empty. I didn't have anything to give."

Both of the boys chose to continue their education in Colorado and spent all their holidays with their aunt and uncle. After receiving their advanced degrees, they both accepted positions in Denver: John as an attorney with a major law firm and David as a high school principal. Ultimately, they both married, John first and later David. Neither invited their father to the wedding. John and his wife had a son that Charles had never met. David and his wife didn't have children, at least as far as Charles knew. David was the angrier of the two and never communicated with his father. John was the one that had made the few calls over the years.

"Have you ever talked to either of the boys about their anger or about what happened back then?" Sarah asked.

"I tried once. John came to town when I had my stroke, but he didn't want to talk about the past. I told him how much it meant to me for him to come, but he implied that he was only there to please his aunt."

"Why do you think they're so angry?" Sarah asked, laying her hand on his.

"They blame me for their mother's death. It doesn't make sense, but they were young. Then I think they believe I abandoned them. I guess in some ways I did," he added softly.

They sat quietly for a while, sipping their coffee. Finally, Charles stood and reached for Barney's leash. "Come on, boy. We need fresh air." The dog raised his head and looked at Charles with drowsy eyes, wagged his tail a couple of times, lifted his rear end into the air, and stretched his front paws as far as he could until all his parts were fully awake. He then got up and eagerly led Charles to the front door, knowing that he was about to have an outdoor adventure. His tail was wagging vigorously by the time he got to the door. Everything was an adventure to Barney.

Later that day, Charles said he was going over to his apartment. "I might spend the night there if that's okay with you."

"That's fine. I'm going to be sewing, and you know how my projects can run into the wee hours." She knew he needed time alone to think things through, and alone time was impossible to get in her tiny house.

"What are you working on?" he asked before leaving. She appreciated that he always took an interest in her quilting. She pulled out the oriental fabrics and the Asian-inspired quilt book and showed him the one she was planning to make. He said he loved it, but there was a sadness in his eyes which made her heart cry. She reached over and kissed him gently. He wrapped her in his arms and stood there quietly for a few minutes.

After he left, the house felt very empty. Sarah reflected on the fact that she had lived there alone for nearly three years, and it had never felt empty until she let Charles into her heart.

Chapter 7

"Hey, Sarah! Stop in when you get back," Sophie hollered. She was dressed in her tattered chartreuse robe and pink elephant pajamas, standing on her porch and waving at Sarah as she was walking toward the park with Barney.

"I'll be there in a few minutes," Sarah called to her. "We aren't going far with this nip in the air." It was early, but Barney had seemed desperate to get out.

Sophie hurried in as fast as her arthritic knee would allow and started the coffeepot. She slipped the package of store-bought sticky buns into a warming oven and headed back into the living room to switch on her electric fireplace. "That looks cozy," she said to herself as she walked back to the door to watch for Sarah. There was a strong wind blowing from the north, and she knew Sarah wouldn't be out there long.

A few minutes later, she saw them coming up the street at a hurried pace.

"Brrr," Sarah said as she and Barney came through the door. She followed that with a deep sigh once she got into the warm living room and stood in front of the fireplace. "This feels wonderful. It actually puts out a little heat, doesn't it?"

"Of course it does! It's a fireplace! Now come sit down while I pour us some coffee and serve these beautiful sticky buns I made this morning."

Watching Sophie pull the buns out of the oven, she couldn't resist saying, "Oh, Sophie. I love your new pans! But they do look just a bit flimsy. What does that say on the side …?"

"Okay. Okay. I got the buns at Keller's Market yesterday. By the way, I saw that woman you used to work with. What's her name? Beverly?"

"She's still there? That woman must be 110 years old by now!" Sarah responded with a grin.

"She's not quite that old, but she told me she intends to work until she drops. She said they miss you there."

Sarah worked at Keller's twice: once when she first graduated from high school and again after her husband died. "I've been gone for four years now. I should stop in and say hello. I just got in the habit of shopping at the market on Main Street. It's so handy …"

"… and it gives you an excuse to stop in the fabric shop, right?"

"Okay. You got me." Sarah responded with a chuckle.

As soon as they were settled at the table with their coffee and sticky buns (and Barney had curled up in the corner with the treats Sophie had for him), Sophie said, "Okay, I have another question for you."

"More questions? Now what?"

"In the middle of the night, I heard a car. I checked my clock and it was 2:45 in the morning! I slipped on my best robe …"

Sarah reached over and lifted the edge of the faded chartreuse pocket that was hanging by a thread and said, "… this robe?"

Sophie gently slapped her hand away and continued. "And you won't believe what I saw. A car had pulled into your driveway, and a man was skulking up to the door."

"Skulking?"

"… and he had a key and let himself in."

"Now, Sophie. You know that was Charles. And you know he wasn't skulking. He was just coming home."

"At that hour? Where had that man been to all hours?" she demanded, looking indignant.

"I'll tell you the whole story if you'll calm down. It's just that he came home because he got lonesome. He went to his apartment last night to have some time to himself, but after a few hours he realized he didn't really want to be alone," she said with a pleased smile. "In fact, I was missing him too."

"Hmm. How disappointing. I expected a better story than that."

"Well, that's good because I have a better story than that for you."

Sophie's face lit up in anticipation. "Yes? So tell me …"

"Charles has decided we won't be moving to Colorado."

"You're staying here!" Sophie hollered with excitement. "Thank the Lord."

Sarah told her friend about their conversation the previous night. "I don't know where we'll be living, but it won't be Colorado. He understands that I need to be near my friends and family."

"So why did he think he needed to be alone last night?"

"He wants to find a way to get on better terms with his sons, and he doesn't know how. I guess he just wanted to think about it."

"He can't think at your house?"

Sarah laughed. "Well he came home, didn't he? I would say that he figured that one out. I sure did. I miss him when we aren't together. I'm not sure how that happened, since I thought I was enjoying my time alone before I met him."

"We people are like dogs," Sophie offered, looking at Sarah's confused expression. "We're pack animals."

"I guess we are, Sophie. I guess we are."

* * * * *

When Sarah and Barney returned home, Charles was sitting in the living room with the telephone on his lap. He looked dejected and glanced up at Sarah without a smile. Barney, highly attuned to the moods of his loved ones, crept over without his usual enthusiasm and rested his head on Charles' knee. Charles gently scratched his ear.

"What is it?" Sarah asked, sitting down on the couch next to him. Charles didn't answer right away, and Sarah didn't push. She laid her hand on his arm and waited.

Finally, he spoke. "I called John while you were gone. I wanted to catch him before he left for work."

"And?"

"He was hesitant, like he didn't know what to say. He just listened, and I talked about wanting to spend more time with him and my grandson. I really wanted to apologize for all the things they think I did wrong, but I didn't. I knew I'd get into trying to justify my actions and I'd say dumb things that would just irritate him, so I just talked about wanting to spend time with them."

"Did he respond?"

"Not right then. He said he wanted to talk to David and that he'd call me back. I didn't expect to hear from him right away, but he called back twenty minutes later." Charles reached down to pet Barney, who was now curled up across his feet. The kitten spotted the movement and scampered over, attacking Charles' hand playfully. Charles smiled wistfully and looked over at Sarah.

Not knowing what to say, she sat quietly, waiting for him to continue in his own time.

After a few moments, he spoke. "He said he'd talked to David, and they agreed that this isn't a good time. He said they're both very busy and wouldn't have the time to spend with me. John said he was sorry."

"Did he suggest another time?"

"No."

Charles dropped his eyes and gently shook his head. "You know, I did the best I could back then. I know it was wrong to throw myself into my work, but I was a mess and didn't know how else to deal with it. When she died ..." He stopped mid-sentence and seemed hesitant to continue.

Knowing he didn't want to talk about his love for another woman, she spoke up saying, "I understand, Charles. When Jonathan died, my children were grown. I don't know what I would have done if I'd had young ones to care for. I was devastated just as you were."

After a few moments, Charles continued. "I made sure they were taken care of. I gave Sylvia enough money to get them everything they needed. I don't know what else I could have done ..."

Sarah remained quiet. She wanted to say the boys needed *him*, but he was torturing himself enough and didn't need that pointed out to him. He was trying to make up for it now, but it was beginning to look like his sons weren't ready.

"Maybe they just need time," she said. "They're still young. Perhaps when they're older, they'll begin to understand."

"I hope you're right," he responded, reaching for her hand.

After a few minutes, he shook his head as if to shake the problem away. He looked at her and asked, "Have you planned anything special for lunch?"

"No," she responded. "What do you have in mind?"

"I think we should go out to lunch and get a whole new perspective on this day!"

"I'd love that," she responded, smiling.

"And after lunch, let's drive around Middletown and see if we see any *For Sale* signs."

Sarah tried not to show her delight. Of course, she wasn't interested in looking at homes outside of Cunningham Village, but looking around Middletown was a step in the right direction.

"I'm with you," she declared.

Chapter 8

As they were driving around looking for realtor signs, Sarah told Charles about a section of town where there were several blocks of Victorian-style homes. "I don't know if they're original, but it would be fun to look at them," she said.

"I don't think we want anything too old that would require lots of fixing up," Charles responded. "But we could sure take a look. Sometimes they're actually newer houses built in the old style. Where is that area?"

Sarah had driven a fellow student home from quilt class the previous year and was fairly sure she could find it again. "Turn here," she directed.

After a bit of wandering, they turned onto Cypress Avenue and were delighted to see a row of colorful old homes with turrets and decorative scrollwork. They drove through the next block as well and were disappointed to see none were displaying *For Sale* signs.

"I'll turn around and drive down the other side of the street. We may have missed one." As he began to make his turn, they spotted an interesting old Victorian house sitting back from the road. There was a brick circular drive approaching the house and a black iron fence around the property; the gate stood open.

The house was not as colorful as the ones on Cyprus, and not as large. It was clapboard painted a grayish green and had brick-red gingerbread trim. Attached to the fence was a realtor's sign stating that it was for sale and giving the realtor's phone number.

"Let's go in," Sarah pleaded.

"It's much too big for us. And it's old. Just think about the repairs ..."

"I just want to take a look."

He shook his head, looking bewildered but took out his cell phone and dialed the number. The woman who answered put him on hold while she contacted the owner. When she came back to the phone, she said that the owner was willing to let them come in, but that she, the realtor, wasn't able to get there until later in the day.

"No problem," he responded. "We'll take a look and call you this afternoon." The realtor, unwilling to leave it that informal, took his name and number and said she would be in touch with him.

"The woman's name is Mattie Stockwell," the realtor said. "She's a little unusual."

"That's okay. We're just taking a quick look. Thanks," and he disconnected.

As they approached the house, Charles immediately saw work that would need to be done, and he again told Sarah he didn't want to buy an old house.

"We aren't buying, Charles. We're *looking*. There's a difference. This will be fun." She knew it was hard for Charles to just experience something for the fun of it.

He needed to be accomplishing a task. *Men hunt, women gather*, she thought, remembering an article she had read on why it's hard for men and women to shop together.

He rang the bell and they waited for someone to respond. After a few minutes, they heard the bolt being thrown and the door began to slowly open. A small, frail-looking woman—who appeared to be in her nineties—peered out. "Are you the people to see the house?" she asked, looking a bit unsure whether she should let them in.

"Yes," Sarah replied as she stepped in front of Charles. She thought it might be less intimidating for the woman to be speaking with another woman rather than a retired cop who couldn't seem to avoid using his cop voice in situations like this. "We'd love to see your charming home."

The woman smiled and stepped aside, inviting them to come in. Sarah was struck by the darkness of the interior. The walls were covered with heavily flowered wallpaper, and the woodwork had a dark stain that appeared almost black. The wood floors were also a very dark color and the windows had heavy drapery. "I didn't have time to open the drapes," the woman said apologetically as she shuffled over to open the drapes on the largest window in the room. "This is my parlor," she said with a sweeping movement of her arm as the dust from the drapery cascaded toward the floor. Sarah coughed as the woman continued. "The dining room is beyond this room, and the kitchen is on the other side. You folks can walk around on this floor, and then we'll go upstairs."

Sarah was more interested in the furniture than the house. "Look at these incredible antiques," she whispered to Charles.

"Excuse my furniture," the woman called from where she was now sitting in the parlor. "This old stuff belonged to my mother, and I always meant to buy new, but you know how time gets away from you."

"*This old stuff*," Sarah repeated softly, shaking her head as she lightly slid her hand over the smooth, glossy finish on the priceless buffet.

After a cursory look at the first floor, Sarah said, "May we see the upstairs?" She felt herself beginning to picture what it would be like to live in this incredible house.

"Don't get too attached," Charles whispered, anticipating her thoughts.

"Yes. I'll come upstairs with you." Mattie Stockwell slowly led them up the staircase.

While they were looking at the room that Mattie called the guest room, they heard a loud bang coming from the first floor. They looked at one another, but Mattie didn't seem to notice it, so they continued their tour.

"What's up there?" Charles asked, pointing toward an open door at the end of the hallway that revealed a narrow staircase.

"That goes up to the attic and the widow's peak."

"Oh! That's sounds exciting!" Sarah almost squealed. "May we go up?"

Again they heard the noise coming from the first floor— this time several loud clunking sounds.

Ignoring the disturbance, Mattie said, "I can't do those steps, but you two can go on up if you want. Just be careful where you step. Some of the floorboards are weak up there."

"I think we'll pass," Charles said, and Sarah looked at him with disappointment. "It could be dangerous," he whispered to her.

Ignoring the continuing disturbance from the first floor, Mattie took them into the primitive bathroom. "Now this room …" Before she could finish her sentence, a single loud bang seemed to shake the entire house.

"Shouldn't we check to see what that is?" Charles asked.

"Oh, that's nothing to worry about."

"I think it might be," Charles responded. "It sounds like your plumbing. Let's take a look."

"It's not that," Mattie said as she carefully started down the stairs. She stopped on the landing and turned toward her guests to explain. "Uncle Hiram doesn't want me to sell the house. I've tried to explain why I have to do it. He'll get over it in time."

"Who's Uncle Hiram?" Sarah asked as Mattie continued down the narrow stairway to the first floor.

"He's my great uncle. He was married to my grandmother's sister, and he built this house back at the turn of the century. The last century that is—not this one. I have papers saying it was built around 1903."

Sarah looked confused. "He built it in 1903? This man must be … wait, he would be way over 100 by now. I don't understand …"

"Exactly! He'd have been 142 this year," Mattie said proudly as she reached the main floor and turned toward the living room. "If he had lived that is, but of course he didn't."

Sarah tilted her head to the side, looking perplexed. Mattie's back was turned as she straightened an afghan on the back of an old rocker, and Charles pointed to his head making circles with his finger as if to indicate this lady was nuts.

Sarah frowned at him and went on. She wasn't willing to let this go. "Tell me about your Uncle Hiram. Why doesn't he want you to sell the house?"

Charles rolled his eyes and turned away from the conversation.

"Isn't it obvious?" Mattie responded. "He built the house, and he wants it to stay in the family. But as far as I know, there's no family to take the house. They're all long gone."

"How do you know that's what Uncle Hiram wants?" Sarah asked, despite Charles' exasperated body language.

"Some people say I'm crazy, and I get the feeling that's what your husband over there thinks." Charles looked embarrassed and shrugged his shoulders. "But Uncle Hiram has lived here all his life and then some. You don't need to be afraid of him. He's a kind ol' geezer. I remember him from when I was a child. He used to keep gumballs in that bowl over there for when I visited." Mattie looked wistful as she remembered those visits. "He was a good man."

Perking up, she added with a chuckle, "… and he still is!"

"Well, Mrs. Stockwell," Charles said, changing the subject abruptly. "We'll be in touch with your realtor. Thanks so much for showing us the house." As they left, they heard another loud bang coming from the kitchen.

"Uncle Hiram says goodbye," Mattie hollered after them.

"That agent was right," Charles commented as they were getting into their car. "That lady has bats in her belfry."

Chapter 9

"Hey, honey. Where are you?"

"I'm back here in the sewing room. I'm glad you're home. I have something to show you."

"And I have something to show you, as well," Charles responded.

He set his bags down on the kitchen table and walked back to the sewing room, trying not to trip over Boots, who was winding herself in and out of his ankles as he walked. "Careful, kitty," he warned. "You're about to get stepped on." Barney came running up about then, and Boots transferred her attention to him.

"Come see these oriental blocks I just finished." She held them up proudly, and he told her it was going to be a spectacular quilt, although he still had trouble looking at a couple of blocks and imagining how it would look as a finished quilt.

"What do you have to show me?" Sarah asked, getting up from the sewing table and rubbing her low back. "I shouldn't sit so long," she reflected.

They went into the kitchen and Charles began unpacking the bag. "I got you a laptop computer today. I've been thinking that we could start looking at houses right here in the kitchen without having to drive all over town." Sarah wondered briefly if her new husband would ever know her well enough to know that she would like to have been involved in this kind of decision, but she decided not to bring up that issue. They were in the process of working out bigger issues. *This one can wait*, she decided.

Once she got a good look at the computer, she was delighted. She sat down and explored the programs that were included. "This will be great, Charles. Thank you."

After dinner, Sarah went back to the computer to send an email to Martha to tell her about the computer. "How do I get onto the internet?" she asked.

"Oh. They'll be here this afternoon to get us both hooked up."

"Both?" she asked.

"I brought my desktop over, too."

"Where will you put it?" she asked, wondering how they could fit one more item into her tiny space.

"I hadn't thought about that," he confessed. "Maybe in the corner in your sewing room?"

Sarah sighed, picturing how crowded that would be, but realized their time in this house was limited. "We'll be moving soon, won't we?" she asked.

"Absolutely. We'll be out by the end of the summer, I would say," he responded.

"Okay. We can manage here for that long. And I guess you should go ahead and give notice on your apartment. It doesn't make sense for us to be making double payments for housing." It wasn't until she got the words out of her mouth that she regretted saying it, realizing that would mean all of his belongings would be coming, too.

"I already talked to the management. I've signed a month-to-month lease. I think we should keep that apartment for now until we're ready to move to our permanent home." Sarah felt her heart swell with love for this very thoughtful man.

"There's a small table in the corner of our bedroom," she called to him. "Get that and set your computer up in the sewing room. There's plenty of room for the two of us."

"What about the stuff that's on the table?" he called to her a few minutes later.

"Just put it on the bed. I'll take care of it later."

That evening, Charles sat at his computer and Sarah sat next to him with her new laptop. Together they searched the listings for relatively new houses with three bedrooms and two baths all on one floor. They wanted a garage and a yard small enough to maintain easily. "We shouldn't be too far from the hospital," she added. "Also, it would be nice to have a park nearby for Barney … and maybe some sort of senior center."

Charles took his hands off the keyboard and looked at her. "You just described our own retirement village," he said with a playful look on his face. "Are you trying to tell me something?"

"Nothing I haven't said before, Charles. Cunningham Village is the perfect place for us."

"But we don't have enough room here."

"And we haven't checked out the houses they're building up on the knoll. Once the houses are finished, they're going to incorporate that whole area into Cunningham Village.

We'd have access to everything we have now, including security."

"I'm not enough security for you? A retired cop?" he teased.

She gently punched his arm. "Stop. I'm serious. I think we should at least talk to the builder and see what they have to say."

Charles laughed, knowing she was going to get her way, but he wanted to keep the game going just a little longer. "But there's no chance of having a ghost like Mattie Stockwell has if we build a totally new house."

"Stop teasing. I'm serious," she said, trying to keep a straight face, but her lip trembled as she tried to hold back her laughter. She knew she was going to get her way eventually.

* * * * *

The group burst into song as Myrtle entered the room. "Happy birthday to you, happy birthday day to you …"

Sarah came out of the kitchenette carrying a yellow cake with lemon icing and two candles: one shaped as an eight and the other a zero. Anna followed her with a tray of cups and a pot of coffee. "We have sodas in the kitchen and water for tea, if you prefer," Anna announced.

Myrtle sat down looking overwhelmed by the attention. "I never expected this …" she was saying as several of the students came over to kiss her cheek.

"I hope you don't mind that I put your age on the cake," Sarah was saying.

"I'm *proud* of those numbers!" Myrtle announced, grinning, and the group applauded.

"You should be!"

After the little party, the group cleaned up the area and immediately pulled out their strips. Sarah demonstrated how to make a precise quarter-inch seam and showed them the different techniques, including a special quarter-inch foot for the machine.

"Can't we just eyeball it?" Brenda Lee asked.

Sarah chuckled. "No, and let me show you what happens when your seam allowances aren't right." She had made a couple of four-patches with inaccurate seams and held them up to show the class the sloppy effect the inaccurate seams had on the finished product.

"Okay," Brenda Lee said. "I get it."

Sarah had brought a few scraps for the students to use for practice, and once everyone was comfortable, they sewed their strips together, pressed them, and cut them into units. By the end of the class, they had completed all of their four-patches and were ready to square them up, cut their larger squares, and begin putting their rows together at the next meeting.

Sarah was glad she had redesigned the class from four sessions to six. Her students were learning what she felt was basic to quality piecing: a precise cut, a precise seam allowance, and careful squaring of the finished blocks.

"How about a ride home?" Sarah asked Myrtle as they were both packing up.

"I hate to be a bother …" Myrtle replied.

By the time they headed for the car, Myrtle was excitedly telling Sarah about the party her family had planned on Saturday. "You'd be welcome to come by, Mrs. Parker."

"It's Sarah," she reminded Myrtle, "and I appreciate the invitation. My husband and I are looking for a house, and we'll probably be out scouring the neighborhoods this weekend."

"Well, feel free to just stop in if you're in my neighborhood. It looks like it'll be an all-day thing, and you'll be able to meet the kids." Sarah noticed how Myrtles eyes were twinkling at the thought of having a full day with her family.

"I'll be there if possible, Myrtle. Thanks for the invitation."

Chapter 10

"Charles, that agent is on the line—the one who arranged for us to see the Victorian house. She wants to speak with us about what we're looking for. Do you want to get on the other line?"

"I got it," he responded as he picked up the extension.

"Hello, folks," the agent said cheerfully. "I'm Charlotte Whitman. We spoke a few weeks ago when you visited the Victorian home over on Cypress. I got your message that evening saying it was more house than you wanted, and I was wondering if I could help you find what you were looking for."

The three talked for twenty minutes describing what they had in mind, and the agent said she would take a look and see what was available. When she called back an hour later, she had identified three houses she would like to show them and asked when they would be available.

"How about tomorrow?" Charles responded as Sarah nodded her agreement. The agent agreed as well and said she would pick them up the next day at 11:00.

Sarah spent the remainder of the day working on her oriental quilt and making some notes for her next few classes.

The next morning they had breakfast and took Barney for a walk before the agent arrived.

"Good morning, Ms. Whitman," Charles said as he introduced himself and opened the screen door.

"Call me Charlotte, please," she responded. Charlotte was a slender blond, wearing white slacks and a navy blazer over a white-and-navy patterned blouse. She carried a clipboard and pulled off the top sheet to show them as they sat down in the living room. "Now this one is a Cape Cod. There's a second floor, as you can see, but the master bedroom and bath are on the first floor, along with another bedroom you can use as your sewing room or den. You can use one of the upstairs rooms for your quests. That way you won't need to use the stairs often."

"We're both able to use the steps," Sarah responded. "We're just looking ahead; we want something we can stay in long-term."

"I'd like to show it to you because it's priced to sell fast. It will require some updating, but it has a small fenced yard for that adorable puppy you have there."

Barney's ears perked up. It had been a number of years since he'd been called a puppy, and he probably had *never* been called adorable—except by his family, who overlooked his straggly coat and wayward whiskers.

"What else do you have?" Charles asked, not overly impressed with her first suggestion.

"There's a rambler over on Second Street that I think you would like. Again, it's fenced—well, the backyard is fenced, and this one's all on one floor."

"How old are these houses?" Charles asked.

"The Cape Cod was built in the late fifties, so it's getting up in years. The rambler is only about twenty-five years old."

Only? Charles thought, imagining the amount of work it would take to upgrade.

"Are there any new homes around? I really don't want to get involved in lots of renovations."

"There are a number of new developments, Mr. Parker, but …"

"Call me Charles," he interrupted.

"Okay, Charles. The new developments are built with families in mind. There aren't any on the market right now that are one story, and they're all big, much bigger than you're looking for." She went on to describe several of the developments being built on the south side of town.

"Oh yes," Sarah spoke up. "We saw those when we were driving out to the restaurant, Charles. Remember the ones on the right side of the road just before the highway? You said they looked so desolate sitting on those big treeless lots."

"I remember," he responded. "That's not for us."

"I didn't think so," Charlotte responded. "And that brings us to the third house, which is in no way what you said you were looking for. But I want you to see it anyway."

"What is it?"

"It's a farmhouse. It's only three years old, and it's built on three wooded acres. Before you object to the lot size, let me tell you: There is a small area around the house that would need to be cared for, but that's all. The rest of the property is wooded. There's a small barn. They were going to have horses …"

"Why is this available? It sounds like someone had plans for it."

"It was owned by a young couple. Unfortunately, the husband was killed in an automobile accident last winter. It was a real tragedy."

After a brief pause, Charlotte asked if they would like to see all three, and they said they would.

They only spent a short time in the Cape Cod; it was immediately obvious that there were too many projects required to get it in livable condition. First of all, the appliances would all need to be replaced. "These look like originals," Charles said somewhat sardonically.

"Well, the house is sixty-five years old, so I would guess they've been replaced a time or two, but I agree they're out of date," the agent responded. She attempted to put a positive spin on the house, but she could tell the couple was not interested. She took them upstairs to see the two small bedrooms that had been added in the attic. Both rooms had sloping ceilings and knee walls with a tiny door to the resulting storage space. One room was clearly the daughter's room with bright pink wallpaper featuring clowns and balloons. The two sons shared the other room, which was papered in minutemen wallpaper and had bunk beds. Sarah marveled that three children could live in such a small space.

"Now that's perfect," Charles announced as they were leaving. The agent was startled by his sudden enthusiasm, but turned to realize he was not talking about the house but an elaborate tree house that had been built in an old oak tree. "Our granddaughter would love that when she gets older."

The next house was the rambler built in the 1990s. "These folks just put the house on the market, and they need to sell fast. They're moving into a retirement community near their children in Kentucky, and their new place is ready. If you're interested in this house, you can probably get it way below asking price." With a conspiratorial look, she whispered, "I'm not supposed to tell you that, but you seem like nice folks."

Charles frowned. It was statements like this that led him to mistrust salespeople.

When they pulled up in front of the brick rambler, they were both pleasantly surprised. The small front yard was landscaped with bushes, pebbles, and mulch. "Very little maintenance here," Charles remarked.

When they stepped past the front door, they were again impressed. The house had been meticulously maintained. The carpets looked like new, and as they entered the small kitchen, Sarah noted the new appliances. "This is a nice house," she said, turning to Charles.

"I agree."

They opened the back door and stepped out on the deck. The small fenced yard was about half concrete patio and half mulch and azalea plants, which were in full bloom. "I would put a couple of benches out there by those plants," Sarah said, and the agent became hopeful.

The shock came when they entered the master room. It was tiny. There was one small closet, no master bath … *and a mirrored ceiling.*

"Gracious," Sarah said, looking up at herself in awe.

"I know," the agent laughed. "The owner told me it was here when they moved in. They always intended to have it removed but never got around to it. The husband said he liked waking up in the morning and seeing that he was still alive." All three laughed nervously and continued to the second bedroom, which was also very small. They left after a cursory look at the basement.

As they were driving to the third property, Sarah asked Charles, "Could you get that mirror down? I wouldn't want Jason and Martha to see that in our bedroom," she added with a slight blush.

"I could get it down, but the real issue, I think, is the size of the bedrooms. That second room isn't big enough for your sewing projects and my desk, not to mention getting a futon in there for guests. Actually, that house isn't any bigger than the one we're in now."

"I hadn't thought of that, but you're right … and we do want three bedrooms."

"I have a second concern," he added.

Sarah, who was riding in the front seat with the agent, turned to look at Charles.

"What's that?" she asked.

"That part of town was a high-crime area when I was with the department."

"What department is that?" the agent asked.

Charles went on to explain he had been retired from the police department for some years, but in his day, there were many drug-related arrests in the area. "We also had a number of domestic violence calls."

"I don't think that's true any longer," the agent assured him.

"I'll check it out," he said.

It took a half hour to reach the third house, which was on the other side of town and a few miles out beyond the city limits. As they approached the property, Sarah was impressed by the beauty of the area. It was wooded acreage, as the agent had described, with a gravel road winding up to the somewhat isolated house. "I would miss neighbors," Sarah commented, "but just look at that adorable house."

Once inside, they found that everything was clean and new. The appliances were modern; the refrigerator had an ice and water dispenser on the door. The floors were hardwood throughout the house, and the walls appeared to be freshly painted.

Walking through the house, they could see that the three bedrooms were of ample size. "This could be my sewing room, and you could have the one next door as your den. Both rooms are big enough for a guest bed, as well."

Taking her hand and moving in close to her ear, Charles said softly, "How about we share the *sewing den* and we put both the guest beds in the other room?"

"A sewing den?" she repeated playfully.

"Togetherness," he responded. "That's the name of the game."

Sarah giggled, again reminding herself that Charles brought out the youngster in her.

"Let's take a look at the barn," Charles said as the agent joined them in the hallway.

As they walked back through the spacious kitchen, Sarah said, "I can see a large oak table in here and our family getting together for Walton-style country dinners." The agent again smiled hopefully.

"Barney would love running around on this property," Sarah commented as they headed for the barn. Once inside, Charles commented that he could make a workshop out of one side, but he wasn't sure what they would do with the rest of it.

"Perhaps we could park the cars in here?" Sarah remarked.

As they were leaving the barn, Sarah noted a wall of cages. "What were these for?" she asked.

"The owners were planning to raise rabbits," the agent responded.

So many plans, Sarah thought sadly. She wondered what had happened to the young widow but decided not to ask.

Sarah got into the back seat with Charles and took his hand. As they drove away, she looked back at the house with melancholy. She loved the property and the house, and for a moment she wished they were young and just beginning their lives together. It was a perfect place to start a family. But it really wasn't right for a couple in their seventies. It was somewhat isolated and far from medical care. *And what if we reach a time when we can't drive?* she wondered. *Wouldn't that mean another move?*

Charles was also thinking about the disadvantages of living so far from other people. He felt a sadness as he thought about the workshop and all the projects he would like to start. *But then I'm getting old, and my aching joints and stiff hands would never allow me to do the things I'd like to do.*

Separately they reflected on the things in life that were no longer possible—the dreams they had to give up as they grew older. But as they looked at one another, they both realized that there were still possibilities ahead, and they had already chosen one of those possibilities: They had chosen to begin a new life together.

"Let's take a look at those new houses they're building in Cunningham Village," Charles whispered to his wife as he was helping her out of the car.

Chapter 11

I t was a warm spring morning as Sarah and Charles drove to the B&H sales trailer to discuss Cunningham Village's single-family–home project and learn what would be involved if they decided to purchase one. Charles pulled up by the trailer, and they headed toward the door just as a man was coming out.

"Good morning, folks." The man was dressed in a rumpled navy-blue suit and was in the process of tightening his tie as he approached the couple. He was heavy, and his hand felt sweaty as he greeted them. "I'm Bill Braxton. Ted isn't in today—that's Ted Harper, the other half of B&H Construction." Sarah and Charles introduced themselves.

"My assistant tells me you folks are interested in buying one of the new homes."

"We're interested in *hearing* what you have to offer," Charles clarified. They went on to explain that they both lived in the Village and were recently married.

After discussing what they were looking for, Braxton responded, "I think you've come to the right place. That's exactly what we have in mind for the community. Have you seen the model home?"

Sarah had driven by it once but only saw it from the outside. They agreed to meet Braxton at the development site on the opposite side of the community where the single-family homes were being built.

As they approached the area, they noticed that a sign had been added: *The Knolls at Cunningham Village.*

"I didn't realize this area would have its own name," Sarah said in an excited tone.

In the northwest corner of the Village, there were a few acres owned by Cunningham Village, which were at a slightly higher elevation than the rest of the community. The property was bordered on the back by a wooded area owned by the city and had been set aside for the future development of single-family homes.

As they were getting out of the car, Charles asked, "How do you feel about having to walk uphill? Braxton said they'd be leveling most of this out, but there will still be an incline when you approach the area from the rest of the community."

"I've thought about that. Walking to Sophie's or to the Community Center would involve a hill coming back, but I'm not concerned about it. It's really not steep, and that slight amount of incline is excellent exercise. I'm more concerned about Sophie coming to our house."

Charles chuckled. "Surely you don't think she'll walk. She doesn't even walk to the Center, and that's less than a half block from her door."

"True. But if we buy up here, I want to make sure our lot is level enough for her to walk from her car to the front door."

"We'll make sure it's level if we buy up here," he said in a teasing tone.

"… if," she added with raised eyebrows.

"Yes. If," he responded. "We need more information about this project and about the builders."

"About me?" Braxton said as he arrived. "There's not much to know about me. I'm just a simple guy with down-home scruples." He dropped his cigarette onto the pavement and crushed it with the toe of his boot.

Charles' antenna went up. He never trusted a person who found it necessary to point out his honesty, especially while littering.

"Let's take a look," Braxton added.

Facing the house, the garage was on the right and attached to the house. The house appeared small from the outside but was appealing. It had light green siding, white trim around the door and windows, and dark green shutters. The door was placed in the center, with two sets of windows on each side. There was a small porch, and someone had placed a large pot of pansies to the side of the single step.

Looking up, Sarah noticed a window near the soffit. "This house has a second floor?" she asked, sounding concerned, but Braxton immediately responded.

"No. That's actually an attic with pull-down steps and a finished floor. Some people want the storage space. It could also be finished for visiting grandchildren."

"Kids would love that," Sarah exclaimed, remembering the hours she and her sister had spent playing dress-up in the attic of their grandmother's country farmhouse. She missed her sister. Mary Bell, older than Sarah, had died many years ago.

Shaking the memory from her mind, Sarah entered the house and found a surprisingly spacious interior. The living room was open and airy, with a fireplace providing a division between the living room and the dining area.

"Wood burning?" Sarah asked and was pleased to hear it was gas.

"We haven't decorated yet," Braxton said, "so you have to imagine these rooms with furniture." There was a card table and four folding chairs in the corner with a pile of brochures and a yellow pad. Seeing Sarah looking at the arrangement, Braxton added with a chuckle, "Excuse the mess; that's my temporary sales office."

Sarah smiled her response and walked past the fireplace and into the dining area. She was surprised to see that the fireplace was accessible on that side as well. "This is cozy," she said, looking at Charles. "We can have candlelight dinners by the fire." He was examining the construction of the unit and nodded his head in agreement. Sarah knew men were rarely excited about candlelight meals, but she thought it would be fun all the same.

Continuing toward the back of the house, Sarah noted that the eating area was divided from the kitchen by a granite-topped island. Sarah walked past it into the kitchen and opened an eye-level oven door, just above the smooth-top stove. She looked toward Braxton questioningly.

"Up there," he said, pointing to the door she had just opened, "that's a combination microwave and convection oven. My wife loves those. That's about all she uses anymore. Your regular oven," he added walking over and opening the two oven doors below, "has a warming oven as well."

"Very handy," Sarah replied, smiling as she pictured herself preparing Thanksgiving dinner for the family.

There was ample counter space and more cabinets than she expected. "This is a nice-size refrigerator," Sarah noted as she opened both doors.

Charles opened the door on the side of the kitchen that led to the garage, and Sarah walked over to take a look. "I like coming directly into the kitchen from the garage," she said. "That's really handy with groceries."

Closing the garage door, Charles walked across the kitchen and opened the back door. He stepped out and Sarah followed him. "A patio would be nice out here," Charles commented.

"Yes, but there's already a small patio over there," Sarah said pointing a few feet away. "What's that for?" she asked, turning to Braxton.

"You'll see in a minute," Braxton replied with a mischievous smile as they returned to the kitchen.

Braxton remained in the background, watching the couple. He could always recognize a potential sale. *These folks are interested*, he told himself with a nod. *At least the wife is.* They had already begun work on the twenty units and, so far, only three had firm contracts.

"How about bedrooms?" Sarah asked, turning to Braxton.

"There are three." Braxton led them from the kitchen through an archway that led to a hallway running toward the front of the house. "All the bedrooms are off this hallway," he said. First they looked at the spacious master bedroom, with its French doors opening onto the small patio on the back of the house.

"Ah! Now I see. What a wonderful place for our morning coffee," Sarah said, looking at Charles for his reaction.

"Nice," he said simply as he checked out the large master bath. There was a shower as well as a large soaking tub.

"Great for those aching joints," Braxton chuckled when he noticed Charles examining it. "And big enough for two," he added with an impish smile, which he quickly dropped when he realized the couple didn't appear to be amused. *Maybe I should save that remark for younger folks*, he thought.

From the master bedroom, they continued down the hall to the other two bedrooms, both small but adequate as a sewing room and a combination guest room and computer room for Charles. There was a second bathroom in the hallway that could be used by their guests.

Arriving at the second archway, this one leading into the living room, Braxton turned to the couple and asked, "So what do you think?"

"I like it," Sarah responded, "but we're still looking in town as well." Braxton started to tell them about the senior services available in the community, but Sarah reminded him they lived in the Village.

"Oh, right. Well, have a seat and let me make a few notes," Braxton said, pointing toward the card table. Sarah sat down, but Charles continued to stand.

"How are you connected to Cunningham Village?" Sarah asked.

"We're contractors. We're developing this part of the community for them."

"Did you build the attached homes over on Azalea, where I live?"

"No. That was all completed before we got involved. The Village contracted with us for this expansion."

While Sarah and Braxton talked, Charles walked back through the house, examining the walls, light fixtures, and how the doors were hung. He opened the electrical box and looked at the connections. In the kitchen, he looked under the kitchen sink and turned the water on and off. When he came back into the living room area, he asked, "May I take a look in the crawl space?"

"Sure. Come on back." Braxton led him back to the kitchen and opened the door onto the small backyard. "You lookin' for anything in particular?" Braxton asked.

"No. Just looking."

Frowning, Braxton asked, "I assume you're retired. What's your profession?"

"Police officer." Charles replied gruffly without looking at Braxton.

About that time, Sarah arrived at the back door as well and asked about fencing. "Sure, you can put in a fence but talk to the homeowners association first. They have a list of approved fences."

"Probably the same ones we use in our section," Sarah responded. She walked around the back of the house while Charles checked out the crawl space.

When they got in their car to head home, Sarah asked, "You were pretty quiet. What did you think?"

"I'm not sure, Sarah. It's a nice house as far as that goes. I like the size and the design. And I like the knoll area. It's somewhat secluded yet part of the community."

"You sound hesitant. Is there something you don't like about it?"

"Well, I'm not sure about the quality of the construction. Some of the work seemed a little shoddy."

"I didn't notice that," Sarah said, not sure what he was referring to.

"It wasn't obvious. It's all on the inside. Under the house, inside the electrical box. I don't know. I just didn't have a good feeling about the workmanship. I'm pretty fussy, though. I might be overreacting."

"Do you want to consider it?"

"Yeah. I think we should consider it, at least. It's a good location for us. If we decide to do it, I'll keep an eye on the construction as it goes up." Charles appeared to be deep in thought but then added, "Yeah, we should certainly consider it."

They had looked at a dozen houses in Middletown and none seemed right. The biggest problem was that they were all older homes and would require work. Most had yards to maintain. "Oh, we forgot to ask about lawn maintenance."

"I read about that in his brochure," Charles responded. "These homes include all the amenities of the Village, including security, road and lawn maintenance, and use of all the facilities."

"That's excellent," Sarah replied. "I liked the layout of the house."

"We can probably ask for changes. Would you like the master bedroom to be in the front?"

"Absolutely not!" Sarah responded emphatically. "I loved that little private patio off the bedroom. I wouldn't want that out front! I want to go out there in my robe for morning coffee. And I want to put a bird feeder out there. We can sit and watch the birds, maybe have breakfast …"

"Don't forget there will be neighbors …"

"Oh. I forgot that. But doesn't The Knolls property run all the way back to the woods?"

"It sure does. Are you suggesting we look for a lot in the back? That's even farther from the Community Center and Sophie."

"It's a few blocks farther—that's all. We can always take the car, but I intend to keep walking as long as I'm able. I think it would be fun to stroll over to the Center for lunch or for a class."

"And Barney will love having longer walks," Charles said thoughtfully. "It'll be about a mile to the park."

"We have lots to think about," Sarah said as they pulled into their driveway. But she knew she didn't have much thinking to do beyond where she would place the furniture. She loved the house and the idea of staying in the Village.

"I wonder if they would do a two-car garage," Charles speculated. With that question, Sarah knew her new husband was giving The Knolls serious consideration.

Chapter 12

Over the next few weeks, Sarah led her students through the process of squaring up their four-patches, alternating the four-patches with the six-inch squares of focus fabric and sewing them into rows, and ultimately adding the borders. Sarah agreed to add an extra class because everyone wanted to learn straight-line quilting.

Everyone was delighted with the results, and they all pleaded with Sarah to teach a second class so they could each make a bed quilt. Sarah said she would discuss it with the shop owner.

Doris had brought in a picture of a Double Irish Chain and asked Sarah if it would be too difficult for her to do. Sarah pulled a pattern book from the rack and showed her the steps. Sarah told her that it would probably be considered an intermediate level but that she felt Doris had all the skills to make it. Doris remained doubtful.

"You might want to look at the Single Irish Chain." Sarah turned to the less advanced pattern and pointed out how similar it was to the throw they had just made. "It's very similar to what we just made but with nine-patches instead of four-patches. It's the arrangement of colors that makes the difference."

Doris was excited when she realized she could make the quilt. She took the book and began looking through the fabrics.

* * * * *

"Are you free for lunch?" Sarah asked. She had called Martha at work, which she rarely did. But it was such a beautiful day, and she really wanted to spend it with her daughter.

Martha hesitated for a moment and then said, "Sure. That would be great. Where shall we meet?"

"How about that café in town, *Le Petit Bonjour*?"

"That sounds very appropriate," Martha responded, "since I haven't had a chance to hear much about your trip to Paris. I'll meet you there in about forty-five minutes, if that's okay."

"Perfect. I'm leaving home now, and I have a couple of stops to make."

An hour later, Sarah and her daughter were seated at a large plate-glass window overlooking traffic. "I wish we had more sidewalk cafés in this country," Sarah was saying. "I think that's one of the things I liked best about Paris. Charles and I walked or took the metro everywhere, and we often stopped at an outdoor café just for coffee and to rest our feet. I loved watching the people and just soaking up the atmosphere."

Sarah had brought a small packet of pictures. She didn't want to bore her daughter but wanted her to see their hotel, some of their favorite spots, and particularly the midnight cruise on the Seine, which had been the highlight of the trip.

"They were playing music; we danced, drank wine, drifted beneath the bridges we've all seen in the movies, and passed by the most beautiful architecture you can imagine." She then dropped her eyes and added with a slight blush, "It was very romantic."

"That's what a good honeymoon should be," Martha said with a chuckle. "Romantic." She had never heard her mother giggle before.

"Charles took this picture of me standing under the Arc de Triomphe."

"I can hardly see you," Martha responded, trying to pick her out of the crowd under the enormous arch.

"Did you go up in the Eiffel Tower?"

"No, but we walked around in that area and went into the gift shop." She searched around in her purse and pulled out an Eiffel Tower key chain. "This is for you."

"Another gift?" Martha said, laughing as she looked at the typical souvenir-shop item. Sarah had brought both the girls, Martha and Jennifer, a beautiful silk scarf from a fancy boutique on the Rue de Passy, billed as the most chic shopping district in Paris. Jennifer, her daughter-in-law, had vowed to treasure the scarf (and the bag it came in) forever.

After their lunch, Martha said she would love to hang out with her mother and enjoy the nice weather. Sarah said she was completely free for the rest of the day. Martha called her office and announced that she was taking the rest of the day off. "Are you okay?" her assistant had asked, not being accustomed to Martha taking time off on the spur of the moment.

They decided to go to Sarah's house and pick up Barney for a walk at the park. Once Martha dropped her car off in front of Sarah's house, Sarah asked her if she would like to see the model at The Knolls first. Martha was excited about it, and Sarah drove them to the other side of the Village, stopping at the sales office first to ask if she could show the model to her daughter. The young woman in the office called over to the construction site and asked the foreman to unlock the model.

Martha loved the house, and she and Sarah talked about where the furniture could go and what Sarah might like to buy new. Martha especially liked the patio off the master bedroom and the idea of stepping outside for morning coffee. Sarah realized she loved it even more this time. They strolled up the freshly paved road to the three lots at the end of the cul-de-sac. "This is the lot I would like," she told Martha wistfully.

"It's perfect," her daughter responded. "Do you think you'll buy it?" Martha asked as they were walking back to the car.

"I really don't know, but I think Charles is coming around. We both love the house, and I think Charles just wanted to know what else was out there."

"Did you see anything else you liked?"

"Nothing that was practical," she responded, thinking about the country farmhouse and her dream of having the entire family crowded around the kitchen table.

They drove back to Sarah's house and picked up Barney for a walk in the park. It was still early, so they walked all the way to Main Street and up the block to Persnickety Place for three ice-cream cones, the double scoop of vanilla being for an exuberant Barney.

Chapter 13

"Let's go buy a house," Charles said as they were eating breakfast a few days later.

"Any particular house?" Sarah asked playfully. She knew he was ready to put money down on the house in The Knolls. He'd been talking about it nonstop all week.

"That one up the street," he said without looking up.

Sarah was ecstatic. "Thank you, Charles!" she said, throwing her arms around his neck. "You've made me very happy!"

He smiled and said, "I'm pretty happy, too. I think you were right all along. The Village has become home."

They dialed the number at the construction site and got the foreman, Max Coleman. "I think the bosses will be in by 10:00. Call before you come just to make sure."

"Thanks, Max. Will you be there for a while? I'd like to talk to you, too."

"I can't sell you a house, but I can answer some of your questions. All I do is build 'em, you know."

"I know, and that's what I want to talk about."

"Okay. Come on over."

Sarah and Charles threw on light jackets and walked over to the trailer. They were met by a tall, muscular man who introduced himself as Max Coleman and led them into the trailer. Sarah picked up a brochure, and Coleman handed them both a sheet with the floor plan.

"Are we able to request any changes?" Sarah asked.

"Sure you can. They'll cost you, of course. Braxton or Harper can help you with that."

"But you know what's possible, right?"

"Sure."

"So, how about the garage?"

"What about it?"

"Two car?"

"Sure."

Turning to Sarah, Charles asked, "What do you think about having a screened-in porch off the kitchen?"

"Will that affect my little patio off the bedroom?"

"No. I was thinking we could have a larger patio there. The porch would open onto the patio and so would the French doors in our bedroom. We could put your little table out there." Turning to Coleman, Charles asked, "Do you do patios?"

"No, but I have someone I can refer you to. He's the landscaper who'll be designing the whole community."

"I'd like to have the larger patio, but let's hold off on the screened-in porch," Sarah suggested.

About that time, a gruff-looking man walked in and gave them an annoyed look. "Harper, I'd like you to meet the Parkers, Sarah and Charlie."

As they were shaking hands, Charles repeated his name. "Charles Parker, glad to meet you." Charles had never liked being called Charlie, especially now that he was retired. "I was Charlie when I was a cop," he told Sarah once. "But I never liked it. My folks named me Charles, and that's the name I want to use."

"Sorry, folks. My day got off to a bad start. Let's get some coffee and start over." He explained that he and Bill Braxton owned the construction company. "We do new homes and renovation here in Middletown and as far north as Hamilton. You've probably seen our signs."

Charles hadn't seen their signs but didn't respond.

"What are you folks interested in?" They spent the rest of the morning going over the floor plans with Ted Harper while Max Coleman made notes. They then drove over to the site in a B&H truck and looked at the lots on the back side of The Knolls. Charles agreed that the one Sarah liked was ideal for them.

"There will be a security fence between you folks and that wooded area," Harper explained. Sarah wondered if she could plant something to climb the fence, maybe ivy or even a flowering vine. She decided not to ask, remembering her friend Andy's theory that it's better to say, "I'm sorry" than to be told no.

By midafternoon, they had signed the contract and received a list of loan companies.

"I squirreled away the money I got when I sold my house," he told Sarah when they arrived back home.

"Yes, and I have my inheritance from Aunt Rose. We're thinking the same thing, aren't we?"

"Yes. Let's not bother with a mortgage."

"Shall we celebrate instead?" she asked.

Charles gave her a hug, actually lifted her off the floor, and spun her around. She threw her head back and laughed. "Sometimes you make me feel like a young girl."

* * * * *

One afternoon as Sarah was working on her oriental quilt, she decided to take a break and look through her book of Asian-inspired quilts. In the last chapter, she found several simple wallhangings. One in particular caught her eye. It featured one large block with an oriental scene and several small blocks down one side and across the bottom. The sashing was black, and the overall look was very striking.

"This would be beautiful in our new home," she told Barney, who looked up at her and wagged his tail, having no idea what she was saying but glad she was saying it to him.

Sarah returned his smile and walked over to the cabinet where she was storing the scraps from her oriental quilt. *This would work for the large block*, she thought, picking up what was left of her geisha panel. She pulled out several other pieces that featured designs she could fussy cut for the smaller blocks. It was a simple pattern and wouldn't take long to make. She sat her quilt project aside and began fussy cutting the squares for the wallhanging. As she cut, she found her mind drifting through the rooms of The Knolls house, seeking the perfect wall for her new wallhanging.

Chapter 14

Several weeks passed before B&H started work on the Parkers' new home. Charles was getting impatient, but Max, the foreman, told him there was a delay with the permits. In the meantime, Charles and Sarah went to the model house where Braxton had moved all the carpet samples as well as samples of siding and roofing. "I like the white siding," Sarah said, but Charles frowned.

"White?" he said rather incredulously. "Why white?"

"Because I want red shutters, and they'll look good with white."

"Red shutters?"

Sarah sighed. "Okay, let's go about this another way. What color do you like?"

"I was thinking green for the shutters."

"And the house?"

"Maybe green?" he responded questioningly.

"A green house with green shutters. Picture it, Charles."

"Hmm. I guess that would be boring. How about a beige house with green shutters?"

"That's an improvement."

"Or maybe gray?" he added reluctantly.

"Gray?"

"A light gray like this sample over here. Don't you like it?"

"I would like it with red shutters ..." she responded, realizing she may have found a compromise.

"Okay. It's a deal," he agreed, smiling.

They went on to look at asphalt tiles for the roof. Sarah said she would leave that up to him, but as he seemed to be settling on a rust-toned tile, she interrupted to point out a dark charcoal that she thought looked best with the gray.

Over the next couple of weeks, they returned to go over the samples, changing their minds several times. "You'll have to make your final decision today, folks," Braxton informed them. "We need to get the supply orders out this week."

"I like the look of the model," Sarah said suddenly, surprising Charles.

"Light green with dark green shutters and white trim?" he responded, thinking about his original suggestion but knowing better than to bring it up. "I like that."

"So do I," she responded. Turning to Bill Braxton, she said, "Make ours like the model."

"Done," he responded.

Once B&H finally got started, Charles went out every day to watch the crew clear the land and do the rudimentary grading of the property for the three houses at the end of the cul-de-sac. Because the Parkers had chosen the middle house and the other two were situated at angles, Sarah and Charles had privacy in their backyard. Sarah had been delighted when she saw the final site plan.

A bulldozer and a backhoe were busily preparing the three sites and digging the trenches for the footings. A few days later, they installed the framing, and Charles knew they would be pouring the footings soon. Unfortunately, it rained for the next eight days and no work could be done. It was a heavy rain, and there were reports of flooding throughout the area. Drivers were warned to avoid entering water standing on roadways.

Charles and Sarah put on their raincoats and boots one afternoon when the sky was becoming brighter and the rain slowed to a drizzle. They put the leash on Barney and headed up toward the site of their new home. The mud was deep and slippery when they attempted to walk over to the foundation. Charles caught Sarah as she began to slip and helped her back onto the road.

"Wait here. I want to take a look at the framing they put in for the footings." Looking into the trenches, he saw they had rebar in place to provide stability to the concrete. He returned to Sarah and told her it looked like the guys were doing a good job.

"The framing looks good. It'll be a long time before they can pour the concrete, though. The trenches are full of mud and water right now. They can't pour until the mud is out of there and the ground is packed solid. It'll probably be three or four days once the rain completely stops."

The next morning, the light drizzle continued and the sun didn't come out until early afternoon. There were still reports of flooding in the area. Sarah needed to pick up a few things from the grocery, and Charles offered to drive her there. On their way, they drove up to the cul-de-sac just to look at their property. Charles was shocked to see the truck there pouring concrete into the trenches.

He jumped out of the car and waded through the mud. Calling out to Max, the foreman, he said, "What's going on here, Max? You can't pour on top of all that mud."

"We know what we're doing here, Charlie. Now move along."

Charles continued walking toward Max, yelling above the roar of the truck. Max pointed toward the road and said angrily, "Get off the site, Charlie. This is none of your concern."

"You need to stop that truck," Charles shouted. "I don't want the footings poured until the ground is ready. You're jeopardizing the stability of my house." Max turned his back, and Charles yelled to the truck driver. "Stop pouring!"

The driver looked at Maxwell Coleman with a questioning look, and Max yelled, "*Pour!*"

Turning toward Charles, Max yelled a string of profanities and ordered him to leave. "Get off the property *now*, or I'll call the authorities." Max's face was red, and he was shaking with anger. His crew had stopped working and was watching to see what would happen. They all knew how Max's temper could escalate.

"I'll call them first," Charles yelled back. "*Stop pouring!*"

Max continued to curse and ordered Charles to stay off the property until the house was completed. "You come back, and I'll be waiting for you," Max threatened, shaking his fist and continuing to spout profanities.

Stunned, Charles turned and waded through the mud and back to the car. His hands were trembling and his face was flushed.

"Are you okay?" Sarah asked, laying her hand on his arm. "What was that all about?"

"I'll deal with it later," he responded. Then, without another word, he gunned the motor and returned to the house to change his shoes. "Wait here," was all he said as he got out of the car and slammed the door.

Still not talking and with his jaw clenched, he drove to the market on Main Street. Sarah had never seen him this upset and didn't know what she should do. She was worried about him but decided she should give him the space to work it out. "I'll be right back," she said as she got out of the car and hurried into the market.

After they returned home, Charles closed himself in their bedroom. He said he needed to think. He was trying to calm down before he took his next step. He wasn't sure who to talk to about the footings.

He wondered if Larry could help him. During his earlier visits to the site, Charles had met one of the crew who appeared to be a jack-of-all-trades. Larry was a middle-aged man who moved slowly but seemed to have the skill to work wherever he was needed. He went out of his way to speak to Charles whenever he saw him. Occasionally, Charles would bring a couple of sandwiches and a thermos of coffee and invite Larry to join him for lunch. They would sit on the back of Larry's truck and talk. Larry's brother was a police officer in Hamilton, and they swapped crime stories and talked about Larry's experiences in the building trade.

Charles decided he would ask Larry's opinion on who he should approach. The next day, he waited until the crew was leaving and motioned for Larry. "How about a beer? I want to run something past you."

Larry looked around cautiously and saw that the bosses had left, so he replied, "Sure," and got in the car.

Once they were seated at the Community Center's sports bar and had ordered their beers, Charles broached the subject of the footings. "Man, I can't get involved in that," Larry said emphatically.

"I just want to know who I should talk to. The foreman? The owners? I know those footings were poured on top of mud, and I'm worried about my house."

"Well, man, if you're really concerned, you should be talking with the folks over in the county inspector's office. They're the ones that approve every step."

"Oh. I hadn't thought of that. That's good news. If the footings aren't right, the inspector will pick up on that and won't approve them."

Larry smirked cynically and said, "You'd think so, wouldn't ya'?"

"That's not the way it works?"

"Not in my town, it don't." Larry took a long swig of his beer and motioned for another.

"Are you suggesting that B&H has the inspector in their pocket?"

"Did you *hear* me say that?" Larry responded with a harsh look. "I didn't say that, and I'm not sure I'd live to see the sunrise if I *did* say that."

Charles was stunned by the intensity of Larry's reaction. "Not live?" he repeated.

"Well, maybe I'm exaggerating just a bit," Larry responded. "But it wouldn't be a good idea to suggest that to anyone at B&H."

"Hmm." Charles was more confused now than ever and didn't know where to go with the whole issue.

"Just let it go," Larry said. "B&H stands behind their work, and you have time to complain if anything goes wrong once you're in the house."

Charles felt little comfort in that and resolved to go to the county inspector's office the next day. Perhaps he could talk to someone higher up. The two friends spent another hour in the bar, talking about the footings and B&H in general. Charles was beginning to wish he'd never heard of B&H Construction. He drove Larry back to his truck and said good night.

"Thanks for helping me think this thing through," Charles said as Larry was getting into his truck.

"This evening never happened," Larry responded.

"Gotcha," Charles replied.

Chapter 15

The next morning, Charles arrived at the County Code Enforcement Office and was directed to the office of the housing inspector. "Hello," the man said, extending his hand. "I'm Kenneth Rawlins. I understand you have concerns about a B&H project."

Charles explained his concern in detail, describing the condition of the ground under the footings the day before they were poured. He had done some research online and was able to be specific about his concerns regarding the footings. "That foundation is critical to the stability of my new home."

"Yes. I hear what you're saying," Rawlins replied. "Some guys have been known to cut corners. I've never known B&H to do that, but let me take another look out there. I'll talk with the guys. Thanks for letting me know." He again extended his hand, clearly calling an end to their meeting.

As soon as Charles left his office, Rawlins picked up the phone and dialed Braxton's private number. "Hey Bill. We need to talk."

"Ken, old man. What's going on?"

Kenneth Rawlins and Bill Braxton went to high school together in the 1980s. They fished, they hunted, and they got into more than their share of trouble. After they graduated, Braxton went to work for his dad's construction company and learned the business from the bottom up. In 2002, he joined Ted Harper, and they created B&H Construction. Braxton brought the knowledge and experience while Ted Harper provided the funds.

Ken Rawlins, working in the county inspector's office, helped them to understand the intricacies of licensing and the building codes. Over the next few years, he was known to occasionally close his eyes to minor violations.

Braxton and Rawlins agreed to meet at Barney's Bar & Grill later that day. Rawlins said he didn't want to discuss the matter on the phone.

"Heinekens," Rawlins said to Sally when she came to take their order.

"Whiskey with a Bud chaser," Braxton said, "and an order of fries."

"Dinner?" Rawlins said sarcastically.

"Rough day," Braxton responded.

After their drinks were served, Braxton turned to Rawlins. "So what's this all about?"

"You need to watch your step, friend. You have a customer who's looking very closely at your work."

"Parker, right?"

"Right."

"And you know this how?" Braxton asked.

"He came to see me."

Braxton threw the shot back and followed it with half the beer. He cursed as he sat the mug down.

"Parker must be talking to my foreman. Max Coleman has a big mouth and doesn't know when to shut up."

"What makes you think someone has to be feeding information to Parker?" Rawlins asked.

"Parker couldn't figure it out for himself. He doesn't know anything about construction. He's a cop."

"A *cop*?" Rawlins shouted loud enough to cause the bartender to turn and look their way.

"Relax," Braxton responded. "He's retired, and he's just one of those old guys without enough to do. He's been hanging around the construction site every day asking questions. I heard Max threw him off the site yesterday. He's probably just trying to get even by coming to you."

"He knows enough to know those footings were poured on an unstable bed. You assured me you'd get the mud out of there."

Braxton swore again.

"Get a handle on this problem, Braxton. I mean it. I'm not going down with you."

"I'll take care of it."

* * * * *

Feeling confident that the inspector would take care of the footings, Charles and Sarah spent the next few days in Hamilton looking at furniture. They had decided to replace a few pieces of their older things. They were going to use Charles' bed in the guest room with a new mattress and replace Sarah's bed with a new king-size bed and mattress set.

They stayed at the Kingston Hotel in the center of town, treated themselves to several nice dinners, and saw a play one evening. "I haven't had that much fun since Paris," Charles said jokingly as they were driving home.

"Let me think: Paris for ten days or shopping in Hamilton for three days. I think I'll take Paris, but it *was* fun shopping with you."

"I thought that young salesman was going to have a stroke when we tested the mattresses. Did you see how red his face was?" Charles asked.

"I think that happened when you pretended to unbuckle your belt, you silly man!"

It was nearing dusk when they drove past the security kiosk. "Shall we drive by the house before we go home?"

"I doubt much has been done since we left, but we can take a look," she responded.

As they approached the lot, they were both surprised to see men on the job. Temporary lighting had been set up. One man was operating a small backhoe and two others seemed to be reinstalling the frames. There were large piles of broken up concrete out by the road. "I wonder what they're doing," Charles said, straining to get a better look.

"I think we should stay out of it, Charles," Sarah said, remembering his last encounter. "Let's just go home." Charles wanted to know what was going on but agreed with Sarah that this was probably not the time.

The next morning he drove toward the property but had no intentions of stopping. He just wanted to know what was going on. That nighttime work was puzzling, although they seemed to be working on the footings. As he approached, he realized the concrete mixer ahead of him was headed for his lot.

"Rawlins must have jumped on B&H about those footings," he told Sarah with a broad smile when he got home. "They have the concrete guy out there today re-pouring the footings."

Chapter 16

Over the next weeks, the crew moved on to the house on the corner at the entrance to the Parkers' cul-de-sac. They were putting the roof up the day Charles drove by. Larry waved to him from the front door. Charles looked around and didn't see Max Coleman's truck, so he parked and walked up to the house.

"You're feeling brave today," Larry said in a ribbing tone. "I figured ol' Coleman had scared you off fer good."

"Not for good, Larry. I've been coming over after everyone leaves. I've been hoping you might be here one night. How's it going?"

"Tough. They gave me a helper a couple of weeks ago—a young college guy, and I had to teach him which end of the hammer to hold onto. What's with kids today?"

"I know," Charles commiserated. "They aren't raised the way we were." Charles stepped between the studs and walked over to where Larry was working. "Okay if I look around?"

"I don't care what you do as long as the boss ain't here, but if you get found out or hurt, it'll be my skin."

"I checked to make sure Max wasn't around, but then I wasn't ordered off this particular property, was I?" Charles said defiantly. Changing his tone somewhat, he added, "When do you think they'll get back to work on my house?"

"The concrete's cured. The mason crew will be here tomorrow to set the crawl space walls, and the framing crew should start Monday with the floor. Once that crew gets moving with the walls, you'll start seeing progress."

"I wish I could see it up close, but I don't want to get Coleman riled again."

"Come on by after hours. I'll be there most of the time, but just go on up now and look around. You know Coleman's truck, right?"

"Sure."

As he walked away, Charles ran his hand over the lumber and turned to Larry. "You aware of any problems so far?"

"Nothing much. That last load of lumber for this unit didn't look too good, but it won't matter. Once the studs are up, they'll do the job."

"Hmm," Charles responded, wishing everything could be of top quality but realizing he wasn't going to get that from a run-of-the-mill builder—or for the price he was paying, for that matter. "Good enough," Charles said reflectively. "I guess that's all we can expect. *Good enough.*"

After Charles left the site, Larry watched him head up the street to his own property. He liked the man and was sorry the builders were giving him trouble. As he turned back to the receptacles he was installing, he thought about the scene the day Braxton ordered the crew to redo the footings on the Parker project.

"What the hell are you telling people," Braxton had yelled at his foreman. "Parker went to the authorities. They could

close us down!" he had screamed. "I'm the boss here, and you have no business ..."*

Larry had unfastened his tool belt and headed for the door. "I don't want to know where this is going," he called to his assistant. "Let's get out of here."

Donald, his young helper, grabbed his toolbox and followed Larry out to the truck.

"Stick your bike in the back," Larry had said, "and I'll drive you home."

"Why did you leave so fast?" Donald had asked as they headed off the lot.

"Braxton's got a temper, and one time he got so mad at a foreman he turned around and fired the whole crew. I need the work."

"Me too. What are they fighting about now?"

"I'm not sure. Something about the guy we're building the house for, but I didn't hear much ... and didn't want to. Let's stop for a beer."

"They won't serve me, Larry, but I'll get something to eat. I forgot my lunch today."

"Oh, yeah. You're just a youngster, ain't cha?" Larry had teased as he passed the Village security kiosk and waved to the guard.

Looking back on that day, he was glad that he and Donald got out when they did. The next morning the guys told him that Braxton had fired Max. Larry wasn't surprised; he had heard the angry tone in Braxton's voice, but he wondered how someone else could pick up in the middle of the project. Later that same day, he'd seen Max Coleman screeching up to the site in his truck. "Quit gawking and get back to work," he had yelled at his crew. *I guess Braxton couldn't figure out how to get along without him, either.*

* * * * *

"Hey, kiddo. I'm driving over to Keller's for some groceries. Do you want to ride along?"

"Oh, Sophie, I don't think so. But could you pick up some coffee for me? I'm getting low."

After they hung up, Sophie grabbed her glasses and cane and headed for the car. She was wearing her new chartreuse sweatpants and matching hoodie and felt very fashionable. Once she arrived at Keller's Market, she was surprised to find the parking lot packed. Sale signs covered the front windows announcing their one-day anniversary sale.

The only basket left in the rack was an oversize one shaped like a truck in the front with a small seat intended for entertaining children. She grabbed the enormous basket, loaded her tote bag into the baby carrier portion, and made her way through the array of sale items precariously situated along her path. Turning toward the vegetable aisle while eyeing the donut display, she crashed into a carefully stacked pyramid of canned peas.

A surprised man standing near the display lost his balance and landed flat on his back as the peas came tumbling down around him. The sign that had been placed on the display landed on his head. Sophie stood speechless and frozen to the spot. *What have I done?*

She looked down at the man lying on the floor among the scattered cans of peas. His wire-rimmed glasses and his bow tie were askew. He had a pleasant round face and rosy cheeks. He appeared to be balding, but it was hard to tell with his tousled hair partially covered by the sale sign.

He wore a rumpled navy-blue suit and one scuffed shoe. The other shoe lay a few feet away. Sophie wondered how he managed to fall out of his shoe. "Are you okay?" she asked, leaning over him as a can of peas rolled off his round belly and hit the floor with a thud.

Remaining flat on his back, the man reached into his breast pocket and pulled out his business card, passing it to Sophie.

Cornelius Higginbottom

Creative Card Consultant

Verses for every occasion

With the help of the manager and two bag boys, Mr. Higginbottom got to his feet. Sophie noticed he was short, only a couple inches taller than she was. He appeared to be in his mid- to late sixties.

"I'm really sorry, Mr. Higgins. I don't …"

"Higginbottom," he corrected with a smile, pointing to his name on the card she was still holding.

Looking down at the card, she read it aloud. "Higginbottom. Cornelius Higginbottom. What do people call you?"

"Cornelius Higginbottom," he responded, looking puzzled. "They call me Cornelius Higginbottom. That's my name."

"Well, I don't have time for all those syllables, so I'll just call you Corny. Are you okay?"

He started to object since he liked his name just as it was, but he said nothing. He had already decided he wanted to get to know this flamboyant woman with oversize rhinestone-trimmed eyeglasses and a matching cane. "I'm just fine," he said with a twinkle in his eyes. "Just fine."

Chapter 17

"I don't know, Sarah. He just looked so cute laying there with cans of peas all around him, and he couldn't seem to take his eyes off me!"

"But Sophie, he's a total stranger. Do you think you should invite him to your house so soon?"

"You're being a worrywart, Sarah. I'll bring him over to meet you sometime and you'll see. He's just an old teddy bear and completely harmless."

"What does he do for a living?" Sarah asked out of habit, forgetting he was in his late sixties and probably retired. "Or is he retired?" she added.

"He's retired from his regular job, but now he writes verses for greeting cards." She pulled Cornelius's business card out of her apron pocket and handed it to Sarah.

"Cornelius Higginbottom? That's a mouthful … and he writes greeting cards? Does he work for a greeting card company, or what?"

"He's a freelance verse writer. I don't actually know much about that yet, and that's exactly why we need to spend some time together; we need to get to know each other."

"Well, Sophie, you're a big girl, and I shouldn't be sticking my two cents in. But this whole thing worries me. You met the man two days ago and already he's coming to your house, and Lord knows what he has in mind."

"That's more than two cents."

They looked at each other and burst into laughter at the same time. "Okay, okay. I won't say another word."

"Would you feel better if you could meet him? You and Charles could come over for a drink before we have dinner …"

Sophie didn't look like she really wanted to share her new friend on their first date. Sarah graciously declined, but she told Sophie they would be home and she should call if she needed them.

Sophie sighed and shook her head as she scratched Barney's ear and headed home. "See ya, kiddo," she called as she closed the screen door behind her.

* * * * *

"Hey, Larry. How's it going?" Charles dropped by one late afternoon to check on the progress of his house. Just as Larry had predicted, the framing crew had made impressive progress over the past few weeks. Larry said it would be under roof before fall.

Charles walked through the house, stepping between the studs and marveling at how small the rooms looked when they were simply outlined by the studs.

"I ain't doing so good, Charlie. This elbow is killing me." Larry had been injured in his younger days when he crashed his motorcycle trying to avoid a sports car that had cut him off on the interstate. "This darn thing acts up when the weather changes."

Charles watched Larry struggling to tighten a pipe fitting between the bathroom studs and could tell he was in pain.

"Where's your assistant today?" Charles asked. "That's a good job for the kid."

"He had to meet with some school folks about something. He told me what it was, but I don't know much about them college things."

"Probably his adviser." Donald had mentioned to Charles that he was looking into changing his major.

"Here, let me do that for you."

Larry handed the pipe wrench to Charles and backed out of the way. "Thanks, man. Just don't let anyone see you doing that." There were a couple of men working late, but Larry had assured him they were okay guys.

Charles took the wrench and lifted it up toward the pipe but pulled it back to look at it.

"Where did you get your hands on this old stillson?"

"Ain't that a beaut? It belonged to my granddad. He was a mechanic up in Massachusetts in the thirties. That thing must be seventy or eighty years old, and it's still goin'. I hope I can say the same about this old body of mine someday."

Charles glanced at Larry and wondered just how old he was. He looked like a middle-aged man who had experienced a very hard life.

Charles gave him a thumbs-up and turned back to the pipe. He carefully adjusted the wrench around the fitting and muttered appraisingly, "This is some tool."

"Folks don't appreciate the old tools like they should. The stores are full of junk now."

Chapter 18

Sophie sat holding the piece of notebook paper Cornelius had handed her.

Another year older and here you are,
No longer young, a fading star,
Balloons and fun are for the kids,
Not those of us who are on the skids.
Happy Birthday.

She'd been asking to see some of his verses, but he'd seemed reluctant. *Perhaps this was why*, she thought. It was, perhaps, the worst thing she had ever read. She suddenly realized the true meaning of the expression *being speechless*. She had no idea how to respond.

"Well, well," she said. "I see you've been writing …"

"This is the way it works for me. Verses just pop into my head. I had to pull over on the way here to write this one down before I forgot it." Sophie wished it had been forgotten.

Hoping to change the subject, she offered him a cup of coffee and said, "My friend was asking me where you sell your verses. Do you work for a particular company?"

"Well, the truth is that I haven't actually sold any yet, but I've only been at this for a few years. Getting published takes time, you know, even in the greeting card game." He took a sip of his coffee and reached for one of the donuts he had brought with him.

"I don't know what to say, Corny. I have to admire you for your perseverance. *There*, she thought, *I managed to get away without responding to that terrible verse.*

"So what do you think of this one?" he asked, looking proud of himself.

"I think those companies will be as speechless as I am when they read it."

"Thank you," he responded with a pleased smile.

They sat for a while enjoying their donuts and coffee. Sophie had the back door open and the room was filled with the pleasant smells of an early summer day. "So what would you like to do today?" Cornelius asked. They had been dating for a month and hadn't done anything but eat so far.

"Let's take a ride somewhere," Sophie suggested. As she waited for his response, she couldn't help but wonder if he had a closet full of rumpled blue suits, or was he wearing the same one day after day. His red bow tie stood askew just as it had on the floor of Keller's market. "Or we could invite my friend Sarah and her husband to join us for a picnic in the park?"

Before he could answer, the phone rang. "Sorry to interrupt your early morning date," Sarah said with a smile in her voice. "I just wanted to see if you and your gentleman friend would like to come for lunch."

Sophie turned to ask Cornelius, but instead put the phone back to her ear and said, "We'd love to."

"What was that all about?" he asked as she hung up.

"We're invited for lunch across the street. I've been wanting you to meet my friend Sarah." She went on to tell him about Sarah and her recent marriage to Charles. He seemed fascinated by the story and asked lots of questions about the wedding.

"Wedding announcements should be more fun," he said suddenly. "That's a wide-open market for a verse writer!" Excitedly, he added, "Do you have a piece of paper?"

You might think we've gone insane,
To tie ourselves to a ball and chain ...

Reading over his shoulder as he wrote, Sophie shook her head and sighed. *I sure hope this man has a pension. He'll never make a living this way!*

Sophie was beginning to wonder if Cornelius was somewhat of a *doofus,* but once she saw him with Sarah and Charles, she knew this guy was much more than his verses. His social skills were delightful, and he quickly made fast friends of the Parkers. Sophie, of course, kept everyone in stitches, and she particularly enjoyed being part of a couple for the first time in many years. As they were leaving, Sarah bent close to Sophie and whispered, "I like him."

"He's like a comfortable old shoe," Sophie responded with a coy smile.

As they were approaching Sophie's front door, Cornelius hesitated as if he had something to say. She sat down on her rocker and motioned for him to sit down next to her. He continued to stand, holding his hat against his chest with both hands like protective armor.

"Sophie, dear, I have something to ask of you, and I hope you won't be offended."

"Yes?" she responded, squaring her shoulders and beginning to bristle. "And just what would that be?"

Feeling apprehensive, he began with a slight stutter. "It's about … about my name."

"And what about your name?"

"I don't like it that you call me Corny." He blurted it out, his eyes searching her face to see how she took it.

Sophie was quiet for a moment, appearing to be contemplating his request. Finally she spoke, saying, "Well, having read your verses, I can see that you might not like to be called Corny. That just might be a little too close to home. What would you like to be called?"

He didn't answer right away; he was still thinking about her first response. There seemed to have been an insult in there, but he wasn't quite sure. Finally he spoke up, saying, "Cornelius. Cornelius Higginbottom. That's my name."

"Okay, Higgy. Unless you're hearing back from a greeting card company, you'll never hear the word *corny* again."

Higgy, he thought. *I don't like it, but it's better than Corny.*

* * * * *

Charles burst in the front door carrying the newspaper. He shouted for Sarah to come see the headline.

"What is it, Charles? You look like you've seen a ghost."

"Max Coleman is dead," he said as he handed her the paper and sunk down on the couch.

Chapter 19

S arah hurried over to Sophie's house with the newspaper in her hand. Charles had just driven off, heading for the job site to see what Larry could tell him. The newspaper had been vague about the details, only reporting that he was found dead over the weekend.

"Maxwell Coleman, foreman for B&H Construction, was found dead on a company job site in Cunningham Village, a retirement community in Middletown." Sarah looked up at Sophie for a moment, and then continued to read. "Detective Frank Oarsman of MPD reported late Sunday that the case is being investigated as a homicide. Coleman had been with the company for fifteen years. B&H has declined to comment."

"*A murder?*" Sophie repeated, looking shocked. "A murder right here in the Village?"

"Who would do this?" Sarah said, not expecting an answer but finding herself actually thinking of several people who might want him dead. They turned the local news station on and sat through the weather and an advertisement for denture adhesive before the station returned to their continuing report on Max's murder. This was the biggest news item the station had carried for many months.

The police chief introduced Detective Oarsman and announced that he would be lead detective in the investigation. Detective Oarsman, a young officer with a very serious look, took the podium but didn't reveal many more details than Sarah and Sophie had read in the newspaper. He did say they had the murder weapon and several leads.

Sarah missed her friend Amanda but never more than at that moment. Amanda was a young police officer and fellow quilter who had helped Sarah and her friends on several occasions over the past few years. She had applied to the LAPD earlier in the year and was delighted to have been accepted. Amanda's parents and her older sister lived in the Los Angeles area and were eager to have her out there, too.

"Too bad Amanda's gone," Sophie said, seeming to have read Sarah's thoughts. "She'd tell us what's *really* going on."

"Maybe," Sarah responded, "but I think Charles will be able to find out. He still has friends in the police department."

About that time, they heard Charles' car pull up. Sarah hurried to the door and motioned for him to come over to Sophie's house. He looked hesitant but walked toward her at an unusually fast pace.

"What did you learn?" she asked before he got in the door.

"Nothing," he responded. "They closed down the work site. It's now a crime scene."

"Our new home is a *crime scene*?" Sarah cried.

"Don't worry. It won't be for long. I'm heading over to the station to talk to some of the guys." Sarah and Sophie encouraged him on his way; they were eager to know the whole story.

As Charles drove out of the community and headed for the police station, he realized it was somewhat of a letdown to be outside the system. Murder was a rare thing in the quiet little town of Middletown, and he would have enjoyed honing his investigative skills. As a detective in Middletown, he had had few experiences with this level of crime. *Maybe they'll let me help out*, he thought, but didn't really expect that would happen.

As it turned out, no one was available to talk with him when he arrived. He waited around for an hour and ultimately had a chance to spend a few minutes with his old lieutenant, Matthew Stokely, who was getting ready to retire. "I don't know much about it, Charles. I understand you knew the man."

They talked for a while about his connection to Max and the house that he and Sarah were having built. Charles asked about Matt's retirement plans and learned he had recently bought a cottage on the western coast of Florida. Matt was eager to begin retirement life. "Retirement's good," Charles said somewhat reluctantly. "Sometimes I miss the action, but life has been good." *Especially since marrying Sarah*, he thought but didn't add.

"How are the boys doing?" Stokely asked. He had known Charles since his boys were young.

"Who knows," he responded. Both men shook their heads in resignation. Stokely was one of the few people who knew what Charles had been though during those earlier days.

* * * * *

Over the next week, Charles and Sarah waited, hoping to hear more. The crew returned to work on the following

Monday and Charles stopped by during the day to see if he could talk to Larry.

"No reason to wait 'til dark now," Larry said. It had only been Max that Charles had been avoiding; the other guys were friendly enough and seemed to have forgotten about the ban.

"What's the word on this?" Charles asked, hoping to hear some of the scuttlebutt.

"I've been questioned a few times, but they don't tell me Jack Schitt."

"They questioned *you?*" Charles replied in disbelief. "Why?"

"They questioned the whole crew. They just asked what we knew, what we saw—you know the drill. You were one of those guys, right?"

"What did you tell them?"

"I told them what an ass the man was and that there was probably folks standing in line to kill him. They didn't think that was funny. Do those guys ever smile?"

Charles shook his head knowingly, and the two men continued to talk about Larry's experience with the detectives. "It felt a little scary, like they thought I might have killed ol' Max."

"Don't worry, Larry. That's the game. They try to make everyone feel guilty, hoping that the one guilty person will break down and confess. A confession is always their best bet."

That afternoon, Charles returned to the police station and was able to meet with the investigating officer, Frank Oarsman. He wanted to offer any help they might need since he lived right in the Village and was involved with

B&H. Oarsman seemed eager to talk with him and asked most of the same questions he had asked Larry.

"You're good at this interrogation stuff," Charles said jokingly as he was leaving the office. "You almost had me ready to confess." Oarsman's expression remained unchanged.

As he was walking down the hall toward the intake desk, he saw Bill Braxton approaching from the opposite direction. A young female officer was accompanying him. "How you doing?" Charles said amicably as they passed, but Braxton didn't respond. *What was that all about?* he wondered as he continued on out to the parking lot.

When Charles returned home, there was a squad car in front of their house. He hurried in and found an officer sitting at his kitchen table sipping coffee. The man stood and introduced himself as Officer O'Brian. He said he had been assigned to the Coleman case and was questioning possible witnesses.

"I just spent a grueling two hours with your boss. You guys need to get together," Charles said with a chuckle. "What can we do for you?"

"Nothing now. I just had a pleasant visit with your wife, and I'm sure Oarsman covered all the questions we had for you." As he stood, he turned to Sarah and said, "Thank you, ma'am. I appreciate your candor. We'll be getting back to you folks if we have any other questions."

Chapter 20

"What's going on next door?" Sarah asked as she approached the quilt shop. There were trucks outside, and workmen appeared to be rebuilding the internal walls.

"I rented it just last week," Ruth responded excitedly. "The bookstore moved out, and they haven't been able to rent it. I offered a much lower amount than they were asking. They must have been desperate—they took it!" Ruth was excitedly running around the shop with a notebook, making notes.

"What will you be doing with it?" Sarah asked, surprised about the change.

"Classrooms! I'm putting in dividers for two classrooms. That way you and I can teach at the same time. Also, Anna is going to teach hand quilting. I keep getting requests for classes that I just can't fill with that tiny little classroom at the back of the shop."

It was true. Sarah knew that a class size of six strained the space. "This is exciting!" she responded.

Looking very serious and laying her hand on Sarah's arm, Ruth changed the subject and asked about the murder. "Did you know the man?"

Sarah explained their connection but admitted she didn't know much in the way of details.

"Is this going to set back the work on your house?"

"Not much. The crew is finally back on the job." Wanting to get away from the subject, Sarah walked over and picked up a bolt of red fabric. "I need a border for my oriental quilt. What do you think of this?"

"I think the color is perfect, but don't you want to stick with the Asian-inspired line?"

"Aren't they too busy? My squares are a jumble of geisha, cranes, birds, lanterns, dragons, koi, and flowers of every description. I was thinking the borders should be very plain."

"I agree, but come look at these tone-on-tones that just came in." Ruth walked back to the oriental display and pulled out a tonal fabric that was several shades of garnet red. "This is an acanthus leaf. I would suggest using a solid black inner border and this with your fabrics. It also comes in black if that would look better. In fact, why don't you bring your quilt top in, and we'll audition several of these tonals?" Sarah was already thinking that she might use the oriental red as a thin inner border and the black tonal for the larger border.

"Perfect. I'll try to come by tomorrow. By the way, when does my next class start?"

"I was looking at September, but let's see how soon the rooms are finished. We might do a late summer class." Sarah thanked Ruth and headed home to have lunch with Sophie.

"Did you eat?" she asked Charles as she greeted Barney and headed for the bedroom to change her shoes. "You remembered I'm having lunch with Sophie today, right?"

"I remembered, but I'm not really hungry. I'm going to work on that doghouse we were talking about. I want to have it ready for Barney when we move." Charles had expressed his belief that Barney would enjoy having a house of his own in the backyard once they moved. Sarah felt certain it was Barney's preference to always be wherever they were, but she decided that building the house would be fun for Charles and maybe Barney would, indeed, enjoy it—especially when they were all outside. With a patio, they would probably spend more time outside than they did now.

"Okay. I'm off," she called to him, and he met her at the front door with a loving kiss and a gentle pat on the rump that made her reprimand him with a giggle.

"Have fun," he called after her.

As she was leaving, a police car pulled up to the curb. *I guess they decided that they need his help after all,* she thought as she hurried across the street.

* * * * *

Sarah and Sophie moved to the living room after enjoying a relaxed lunch in Sophie's kitchen. Sophie turned the television on, and Sarah placed their coffee cups on the Log Cabin coasters she had made for Sophie at her quilt club the previous week.

Sophie was still standing near the television when Sarah said, "Could we watch the news for a few minutes, Sophie? I didn't have time to read the paper this morning."

Sophie picked up the remote and switched to the local news channel. "This channel?" she asked.

"I was actually hoping for some national news, but ..." She stopped in the middle of her sentence, shocked to see

Charles' picture flash onto the screen. "Wait!" she shouted. "Listen!"

The words at the bottom of the screen read "Breaking News" and the anchorman was speaking.

"Local resident and retired police officer, Charles Parker, was arrested today for the murder of Maxwell Coleman, foreman with B&H Construction. The body was discovered Sunday morning on the construction site where Parker was having a home built. Stay tuned for more on this …"

Sophie reached for Sarah just as she began to collapse. She was able to guide her onto the couch so she wouldn't fall to the floor. All color had drained from Sarah's face as she muttered, "Oh, Sophie, this is all my fault."

Chapter 21

"**I**t's not your fault, Mrs. Parker."

Sarah received the call from Graham Holtz within moments of returning home from Sophie's house. Graham was an attorney and long-time friend of Charles. He explained that he received a call from Charles and was on his way to the police station, but first Charles wanted him to call her. "He said to tell you it's all a mistake, and he'll be home as quickly as we can work this out."

"Of course it's a mistake," she said impatiently. "But why do they *think* he's guilty? I shouldn't have told that officer about the problems with the house. He just got me talking, and before I knew it …"

"They didn't arrest him because of anything you said, Sarah. I spoke with the prosecutor's office just a few minutes ago. They have his prints on the murder weapon and some other incriminating evidence that I don't know about yet. I'm on my way to find out everything and see Charles."

"Incriminating evidence? How can that be? You know Charles, and you know as well as I do that he's innocent!"

"Of course he's innocent, Sarah. Of course he is." Graham tried to sound confident, but he too was worried. He didn't share it with Sarah, but he was also told there were witnesses to threats being made during an argument between Charles and the victim. "I'll find out what's going on, and I'll let you know the minute I know something."

"When can I see him?"

"Not until he's been booked and processed. I'll be with him the whole way, and I'll call you when I know something. Just sit tight. Give me your cell number in case you go somewhere."

Sarah gave him the number but added, "I won't be going anywhere except to see Charles."

Barney's tail and ears were so low they were practically dragging the ground. Even little Boots had curled up on top of the refrigerator and quietly watched Sarah with apprehension. "It's going to work out. You'll see," she reassured them both in an attempt to reassure herself.

An hour later, and still no word from Graham Holtz. Sarah called his office and got voice mail. "Enough waiting," she said aloud and grabbed her sweater. She called her daughter Martha to see if she would go to the police station with her, but there was no answer there, either. "Doesn't anyone stay home anymore?" she grumbled as she grabbed her car keys and ran out to the car.

"Wait for me!" she heard as she was starting the car. Sophie was tapping her cane across the street and heading for the passenger door. "I'm going with you," she said as she arranged herself on the seat and struggled to get the seat belt across her hefty body. Sarah started to object, but Sophie was clearly hearing none of it, and she was relieved to have someone with her. "Let's roll," Sophie announced.

When they arrived at the police station, it was late afternoon. Shifts were changing, and the desk sergeant made several calls in order to track down Charles' current location in the system. "He's being booked," the sergeant said kindly. "You can sit over there." He then added, "He'll be okay, Mrs. Parker. He's a good man."

"You know my husband," she responded, looking thankful.

"You bet I do. I know his attorney, too. If it can be done, Graham Holtz can do it. Charlie's in good hands." She wasn't used to hearing her husband be called Charlie, but she was glad so many of the officers knew him.

"He's innocent, you know," she said softly as she walked away. When she turned to sit down, she saw that he was nodding his head reassuringly.

Sarah and Sophie sat on the bench for an hour waiting to see someone, hopefully Charles or Graham. A tall detective dressed in tan slacks and a navy blazer stepped in the lobby and looked around until he spotted the two women. "Mrs. Parker?" he asked, looking at Sarah.

"Yes? Can you tell me what's happening with Charles?"

"His attorney will be out to see you in a few minutes, and the two of you will be able to meet with Mr. Parker."

"The two of us?" Sophie asked eagerly.

"No, I'm sorry. Just Mrs. Parker and the Parkers' attorney."

"I hate to leave you here alone, Sophie."

"I'm starving," she responded. "I'm going to walk across the street to that little sandwich shop. If I'm not here when you come out, I'll be there, okay?"

"Of course. I hope we won't be long."

"I hope you stay as long as it takes. I want Charles to be in that car when we go home."

But Sarah and Sophie went home without Charles. Sophie drove the car because Sarah couldn't stop sobbing. When she got home, Sarah called Martha and Jason to let them know what was happening. Martha had been at work and knew nothing about the arrest; Jason heard it on the 5:00 news and had left numerous messages on Sarah's machine.

Sarah took a shower and tried to eat a bowl of soup, but her throat immediately tightened up as she lifted the spoon; she poured it back in the pan and stuck the pan in the refrigerator. *Maybe later*, she told herself. She wondered if Charles had eaten.

Around 9:00, the phone rang and she jumped. She felt the anxiety in her stomach as she hurried to the phone.

"Sarah? It's Graham. How are you holding up?"

"I can't even answer that question, Graham. I must be in shock; I can't seem to think straight."

"That's normal. You'll have to take this moment by moment. I just left him, and he'll have the night to rest up. They won't be bothering him again until morning. They've scheduled his arraignment for 9:00 in the morning."

"What does that mean, and can I be there?"

"The prosecutor will read the charges, and Charles will plead not guilty. Sarah, I'll be there with him, and you wouldn't be able to speak to him. I would suggest you not put yourself through it."

"What if they let him out?"

"I'll be asking for bail, but he may not get it."

"But if they do, I want to be there to bring him home."

"I understand. Do you want me to pick you up?"

"No. I'll call my son. Thank you, Graham. I know you'll do what's best for him."

After they hung up, she dialed Jason and told him about the arraignment. Before she had a chance to ask him, he said he'd pick her up at 8:15.

Not able to face any more of the day, Sarah went to bed, knowing she wouldn't be able to sleep. She played back the meeting at the police station in her mind, wishing she had known what to say to raise Charles' spirits.

Charles looked haggard in his orange jumpsuit. The sight of handcuffs made Sarah want to cry, but she held back for his sake. She and Graham sat across the table from Charles, and when he reached for her hand, the guard started to move. Graham gave the guard a pleading look, and the guard shrugged and moved back against the wall. Charles and Sarah held hands throughout the meeting.

"So what's this all about, Graham?" Charles asked. "What do they think they have on me?"

"They have your prints on the murder weapon."

"The stillson pipe wrench, right?" Charles asked.

"Right," Graham responded, looking worried. The specifics of the weapon had not been released.

Charles told him about the day he helped Larry tighten the pipe. "What else?"

"They have several witnesses who identified you during that lineup earlier. They saw you in a heated dispute with Coleman, and they heard threats being made."

"Threats? There were threats all right, but Coleman threatened me! Not the other way around!" Charles was getting heated, and Graham assured him they would be going over every detail of the evidence and his responses.

"Right now, just let me tell you what they have."

"Sorry," Charles said contritely. "Go on."

"The county building inspector reported that you seemed to be out to cause problems for B&H."

"What?"

Graham raised his hand, indicating that Charles should wait and listen. "We don't have much time, Charles." He went on to say that there were other reports of ill feeling between Charles and Coleman, "but the main issue is the murder weapon, and we need to confirm where you were the day he was murdered."

"Sarah?" Charles said, looking toward his wife. "Do you remember where we were?"

"I taught that one-day class at the quilt shop. I think you went to the lumberyard to get materials for the doghouse, didn't you?"

"No. I didn't go that day. I remember now; I was tired, and I took a nap in the afternoon and watched the game off and on."

"Alone?" Graham asked.

"Yes. Alone," Charles responded. His shoulders dropped, and he looked defeated already.

"We're going to beat this, friend," Graham Holtz said as he stood. "Hang in there. Hopefully you'll be at home this time tomorrow night."

Sarah returned to the present time with a start, noticing by the bedroom clock that it was now 4:00 a.m. She got up and made a pot of coffee, knowing that sleep would not be coming to her that night. The phone rang just as the coffee was ready. Sarah looked at the clock and saw it was only 4:20. Her heart sank anew, fearing what else might have happened.

"Hi, kiddo. Why are your lights on so early?"

"I can't sleep."

"Neither can I. I'll be right over."

Chapter 22

T he judge looked at Charles and raised one of his bushy eyebrows. "Detective Parker. I never expected to see you at the defense table."

"This is a good sign," Jason whispered to his mother. "The judge knows him."

Over the next few minutes, the prosecution presented their charges, and Charles responded not guilty.

The prosecution recommended setting bail at $500,000. Before the defense attorney could speak, the judge roared, "Nonsense. Detective Parker has served this county with honor for several decades." He turned his head toward Parker's attorney and again raised his eyebrow.

"Thank you, your honor," Graham Holtz said. "Detective Parker is indeed a decorated officer, now retired from the MPD. He is not a threat to the community, and he is not a flight risk. Being newly married and in the process of building a new home, he has strong ties to the community. I might add that all evidence against Detective Parker is circumstantial. We request that Detective Parker be released on his own recognizance." Taking his lead from the judge, Graham began referring to Charles as *Detective* Parker.

"Well, that's perhaps going too far in the other direction considering the severity of the charges. I'm setting bail at $100,000. Good luck, Detective Parker," he added and pounded his gavel. "Next case."

Sarah looked at Jason, somewhat confused. "Is this a good thing?"

"I think so. I just hope *this* judge hears the case if it goes to trial."

Sarah caught Charles' eye just as he was being led from the room. She hurried toward Graham, but he put his hand on her back and directed her out of the room and into the hallway.

"Well," he said. "That's the first step. I'll help you arrange for bail, and we'll get your fellow home. Then the real work begins."

* * * * *

"I wrote this verse for Sarah. If I could draw, I'd make her a card," Higgy announced proudly.

"I have some cards that are blank inside," Sophie said, reaching for her box of cards. "Show me your verse."

Sorry your guy has landed in jail,
Without even the chance of bail,
But don't you fret,
Things'll get better yet,
And he'll be home eating kale.

Sophie moaned. "Perhaps we should just tell her how we feel, Higgy. Besides, he's out on bail now."

"I know, but that doesn't rhyme."

Sophie started to slide the blank card back into her desk, but he stopped her.

"No. Don't put that away. I'll write my verse on the inside, and you can give it to her."

While he carefully penned his atrocious verse, Sophie shook her head, wondering where this man got the idea he could write verses.

Later, while they were having lunch, she nonchalantly asked, "How did you get started writing verses, Higgy?"

"Well, it's an interesting story. I had this girlfriend when I was in high school. She didn't really know she was my girlfriend, but that's another story." Sophie wondered about that other story.

"One day she came to school and her eyes were all red. I was embarrassed to ask her what happened; I'd never really talked to her. But later I heard her talking to her friend. Her dog was dead. Got hit by a car." He stopped and looked up at Sophie, as if that were the end of the story.

"Well that's too bad, but what does that have to do with verses?"

"Oh. I wrote my first verse that day." Again, silence.

"And …?" she asked impatiently.

"Well, it went something like this: Roses are red, apples are too. It makes me sad when you're so blue. Boo-hoo."

Sophie gulped. "I see. So that's how she found out she was your girlfriend?"

"Oh no; I never told her that. But I started writing verses everywhere—in my notebook, on the edges of my test papers, on napkins, wherever there was a place to write. My mom said I was an *artist with words*. I loved hearing that, and I just kept writing."

"Your mother liked your verses?" Sophie thought about that, realizing that some mothers were totally blind to their children's shortcomings. "So that's the whole story?"

"Yes, that's about it. I kept writing them, and after I retired I decided to sell them. I had five boxes of verses by then. A couple of years ago, I pulled up a list of greeting card companies on the internet, and I started sending the verses to them."

"And you haven't sold any?"

"Not yet. These things take time, you know."

Sophie marveled at his persistence, but her thoughts were interrupted by the sound of a car pulling up across the street. She hurried to the front door and was overjoyed to see Charles getting out of the car, along with Sarah and her son, Jason. "Thank the Lord," she whispered.

* * * * *

Jason shook Charles' hand, wishing him luck, and kissed his mother on the cheek. As he was leaving, he saw Graham Holtz pulling up to the curb. "Your lawyer's here," he called over his shoulder.

Sarah put the coffeepot on and started slicing ham for sandwiches. She hoped to get their home life back to a semblance of normal as quickly as possible for Charles' sake. "Come on in," she called to Graham when she heard him tap on the screen door. "We're in the kitchen."

While she prepared lunch, the three refrained from talking about Charles' arrest. Instead, Graham asked about the new house and Charles drew a quick sketch of the layout. "It's perfect for the two of us, and we can even accommodate an occasional guest."

Barney had been holding back; he was still worried about the tension in the air. Boots, on the other hand, seemed happy to have everyone back home and was enthusiastically attacking Graham's shoestrings.

After lunch had been cleared away, the three remained sitting around the table, and Graham pulled a yellow pad and a file out of his briefcase. "Let's take their so-called *evidence* one at a time."

Starting with the fingerprints, Charles retold his story about helping Larry tighten the fittings using the stillson pipe wrench. "Have you seen other people using the wrench?" Graham asked.

"Not when I was there. I think you should talk with Larry about that. It's his wrench, and he would know who's used it. I only know he's protective of it; it belonged to his grandfather." Graham made a note to talk with Larry.

"Now. How about that argument? Who was involved and what was it about, from the beginning." Charles again, but in minute detail this time, told how he discovered the mud in the trenches and what happened the day he arrived and found that they were pouring the concrete footings anyway.

"What about threats?"

"As I recall, my only threat was that I would contact the authorities. Coleman said something like, 'Come back on this property, and I'll be waiting.' I'm really not sure of the exact words."

"No specific threats of bodily harm were made?"

"None. I don't know what Coleman might have said to his crew after I left."

"That's a good point. That might be where the so-called witnesses heard threats. I'll explore that possibility with them. If they weren't made in your presence, they're irrelevant to the trial. I'm concerned that you don't have an alibi for that day." He waited for Charles to speak.

"What can I say? I was home alone. I don't have any way to prove that."

"I'm not too worried," Graham said as he was picking up his papers an hour or so later. "Everything is circumstantial. What we need is another suspect. Any ideas?"

"Not off the top of my head, but then I really didn't know the man well enough to know if he had enemies. He could be pretty nasty and probably ticked off a lot of people. Are the police still investigating?"

"You know the answer to that better than I do. But in my experience, once they have a suspect locked up, they don't go looking for more."

"My experience, too," Charles agreed, looking discouraged.

"I don't have to tell you how important it is that you stay away from the witnesses, right?"

"Right," Charles responded without much conviction.

"Charles, I mean it. Stay away from the jobsite and anyone associated with it. I know it's your nature to want to investigate, but this is *not* the time for you to do it." Graham added that he would have his own investigator look around.

Charles saw Sarah's eyes light up, and he knew what she was thinking. He didn't want to bring it up in front of Graham, but he knew he would have to talk to her about not doing any of her own clandestine investigating. *Whoever killed Max Coleman would willingly kill again.*

Chapter 23

I t had been almost a week since Charles' release on bond. Sarah and Charles sat in the living room as they had most afternoons that week. Charles was in his recliner facing the television; the channel was set to one of his favorite sports, baseball. Sarah, sitting on the couch, thumbed nonchalantly through a quilting magazine. To an observer, they could be any couple quietly settling into married life.

But closer observation would reveal that Charles, though appearing to be watching his favorite team play, was not responding when runs were made nor when his favorite batter struck out. And Sarah, although diligently turning the pages of her magazine every few minutes, was totally unaware of the words printed on the pages.

Both were in their own worlds searching for answers, trying to come up with a plan, fearing the future, and feeling helpless and alone.

Charles wanted to put on his badge and gun belt and head out on the streets like he did when he was a young officer. He wanted to track down and handcuff the man who killed Coleman and turn him into that arrogant young

Detective Oarsman. He wanted to say, "See, kid? This is how it's done."

Sarah wanted to go back to that time a few weeks before when she was a new bride and had an adoring husband, when they laughed and touched and planned. She wanted their life back, and she was willing to do whatever was necessary to get there.

Where Charles may have been daydreaming, Sarah was devising a plan.

* * * * *

"Is there someone working here by the name of Larry?"

"Who wants to know?" the man asked.

"I'm Sarah Parker. My husband …"

"Ah, yes! You're Charlie's wife. I was sorry to hear what's going on with him. Is he home now?" Before Sarah could respond, the man added, "By the way, I'm Larry."

Sarah smiled a relieved smile. Larry appeared to be friendly and easy to talk to. She'd been nervous about going to the jobsite after all the problems Charles had there.

"Yes, he's home," she responded with a sincere smile. "And I need your help. I was wondering if you and I could talk sometime."

"I'm happy to do anything I can to help my buddy. He's a good man." Looking around, he added, "You know … things are pretty quiet around here right now. Why don't I tell these guys I'm going to lunch with a pretty lady?"

Sarah smiled and thanked him. She was determined to help Charles clear up this mess no matter what it took, and it looked like Larry just might be willing to help her do that. "Let's take my car and go up to the Community Center.

They have a nice lunch buffet there on Fridays. My treat," Sarah said.

"Well, well. That would be really nice. I'm pretty dirty, though," he said looking down at his soiled jeans.

"No problem. You can wash up at the Center, and the jeans don't matter. You'll see when you get there." Sure enough, there were several men from B&H there already, as well as a group of very elderly women in bibs who were enjoying a field trip with their nurses.

"I fit right in," he said with a snicker as he headed for the men's room.

Once they filled their plates from the buffet and sat down across from one another, Larry spoke up, asking, "So how do you think I can help?"

"The obvious thing is the wrench. That seems to be their primary piece of evidence."

"They talked to me about that, and I told them all I know. Charlie held it once, Donald my assistant uses it sometimes, and of course me. I don't know of anyone else's prints that should be on it. They wouldn't tell me anything. Does it have other prints?"

"Our lawyer said there are some other prints, but they're smudged and unidentifiable."

"So why did they pick out Charlie? Why didn't they arrest me or Donald?"

"That's because of the argument they had about the footings. I guess some of the guys you work with told the police that Charles threatened Max."

"He did no such thing," Larry responded irately. "I was right there." Larry shook his head and added, "Whoever said that was either mistaken or lying to cover for somebody. I'll ask around and let Charlie know."

"I'll tell you the honest truth, Larry. Charles doesn't know I'm here, and he forbid me to get involved. But I don't think he stands a chance of being cleared unless someone finds the person who killed Coleman. His lawyer stressed the importance of Charles staying away from the witnesses. I should probably stay away from them, too, but maybe you could ask around?"

"Sure. I don't know what I can find out, but at least I'll see what the guys have been saying. I want them to be clear on what was said before they're asked to testify."

"Do you have any idea who would want to kill Coleman?"

"Well … let me see now." Larry looked up as if he were doing a mental calculation. "Yeah, I would say that would be probably everyone he ever met!"

"He's that bad?"

"He was unpredictable and full of anger. And it came out when you least expected it. When you put him with Braxton, who's volatile himself, we were walking on eggshells around here."

"Hmm. I wonder about Braxton. Did they get along?"

Larry dropped his eyes and fiddled with his napkin.

"You have something you want to say, don't you? Go ahead, Larry. Please. We've got to get my husband out of this mess."

Larry was hesitant but decided to go ahead and tell her about the day he and Donald left the jobsite to avoid witnessing a blowup between Braxton and Coleman.

Still fiddling with the napkin that was now folded into what looked like a sailboat or a chef's hat, Larry took a deep breath and began talking. "Well, a few weeks before the murder, Braxton was shouting at Max ... something about him mouthing off to the customer—Charlie, I guess. It was right after Charlie went to the inspector. I don't know what went on since Donald and I grabbed our stuff and skedaddled. I only know Braxton was fuming."

"I'm hesitant to talk with Braxton myself, and I don't think you should. You could lose your job."

"You bet I could—and *would*—if I started asking Braxton questions."

"I might talk to the inspector. Do you know his name? I can't ask Charles."

"Rawlins, I think. He's in the county offices over on Main Street. Building inspector. But I gotta tell you, he's real tight with Braxton. *Real* tight."

"Charles said he thought the inspector might be in B&H's pocket."

"Smart guy, your Charlie."

Larry went back to the buffet for a couple of desserts, and Sarah got them both coffee. "This has been nice, ma'am. I don't cook much, so most of my meals are sandwiches. This was real nice!"

Sarah gave him her cell phone number. "If it's not on, just leave a message. Charles doesn't bother with my phone, and I don't want him to know I'm looking into this."

"Well don't get me in trouble with him. He's been a good friend to me."

"We're being good friends to him, Larry. If we can get him cleared, he sure can't be upset with us."

"Good point."

When she got home, Sarah stopped at Sophie's house and told her about her conversation with Larry. "I don't want anything laying around the house for Charles to see. Could I leave my notepad over here? I'm starting to collect some names and a few facts."

"I have a better idea. I'll put all this on 3 × 5 cards like that detective gal out in Santa Teresa does. That way we can sort them and rearrange them until the answer pops out! At least, that's the way it works for her." Sophie loved her mysteries, particularly the lighter ones featuring female detectives with spunk. Sarah suspected Sophie pictured herself in those novels.

"Great idea, Sophie! I'll let you know when I hear back from Larry. In the meantime, do you want to go with me when I go see the building inspector?"

"Do I look like I would miss an opportunity like that?"

When Sarah got home, Charles had turned off the television and was in the backyard with Barney, sitting on the bench looking at the pile of wood he had purchased for the doghouse.

"Just what I needed," he said with a weak smile as she came out of the door carrying two glasses of zinfandel and a basket of chips.

"Would you like to go out for pizza tonight?" she asked.

He nodded his response as he tapped her glass with his.

"To making it through this," he toasted.

Chapter 24

"Larry, I'm glad you called. I wanted to ask you something, but what do you have for me?"

"I wanted to let you know that I talked to the guys. It looks like there were only two of them talking to the cops. They both admitted to me that all the threats they heard were made by Max, and they were made after Charlie drove away. At one point, Max said, "If that guy shows his face around here again, he's a dead man." It was all Max, like I said. The only threat anyone heard Charlie make was when he threatened to call the police."

"Thank goodness. This should help."

"Yep," he continued, "and one of the guys said he'd clear it up with the prosecutor's office. The other guy is afraid to go near the station. I think he's wanted somewhere. It wouldn't surprise me if he disappears before the trial. And when they call me on the stand, I can clear it up, too. That blows a hole in their case, at least."

"I'll let our lawyer know. He'll be talking to the guys, too. Now I'd like to talk to Donald sometime. When does he work?"

"Donald quit a couple of weeks ago. He's going to school full time now."

"Do you know where he lives?" Sarah asked.

Larry thought for a moment but then remembered. "I drove him home one night. I'm pretty sure I can find it. Do you want me to take you over there? He might be in class, but I think he has roommates."

"Would Saturday be okay? I know you don't work that day, but …"

"Actually, Saturday would work for me. I'm off but I'll be coming over here to meet the plumber around 9:00. I should be free by 11:00 or so."

"I'll follow you in my car so you can go on home," Sarah suggested.

"Great. Won't Charles wonder what you're doing?"

"I'll tell him I'm shopping. I hate having to lie to him, but I keep telling myself it's for his own good. I'll be here at 11:00 unless I hear from you."

When she got home, Sarah grabbed Barney's leash and crossed the street to Sophie's door. "Do you want to go shopping with me on Saturday?"

"Shopping? I guess. What are we shopping for?"

"A killer," Sarah responded, causing Sophie's eyes to fly open like two saucers. "Actually, we're going to see if we can find Donald, Larry's assistant. I want to ask him some questions."

"Donald?"

"Oh, sorry. I forgot to tell you about Donald. Larry's that friend of Charles' who's working on the house. I told you about having lunch with him the other day."

"Yes, but who's Donald?"

"He's Larry's young assistant. A college student. I'm hoping Donald might have seen or heard something that would help clear Charles."

"Sounds like fun. Does Charles know we're going to be *detecting*?"

"Absolutely not!"

"Ah … then this is a phony shopping trip you're inviting me on."

"We'll do a little shopping; I don't like to be *totally* untruthful with Charles."

"I see your point. Well, whatever you're planning, count me in."

* * * * *

"Knock louder," Sophie suggested. "Young people sleep late."

"It's noon. Surely they're up by now."

At that moment, they heard the dead bolt turn and the security chain being removed. A young girl, probably in her late teens, opened the door a few inches and looked out but quickly covered her eyes when the sun hit her face. Her hair was mussed, and she appeared to be wearing an old rumpled tee-shirt and underpants. Her feet were bare.

"Yes?" she said, sounding confused as to who was at her door and possibly what planet she was on.

"Sorry to disturb you," Sarah said politely. "We're looking for Donald Wasserman. Is he home?"

"I don't know. Hang on." She left the door ajar and walked away. They heard her yelling for Donald, and after a while she returned to the door. "I guess not. Who are you?"

"We just want to speak with him about his job in Cunningham Village. I wanted to …"

"Oh, he doesn't work there anymore," the disheveled girl interrupted.

"I realize that, but I still need to talk to him. Do you know when he'll be home?"

Before the girl could answer, a deep voice bellowed from somewhere upstairs. "Who is it, Amy?"

"It's a couple of old … it's a couple of ladies who want to talk to you about Cunningham Village."

"What about it?" he called from the upstairs banister.

Sarah called up to him. "Please, just a few minutes."

"Hang on," he replied.

The girl closed the door, and Sarah looked at Sophie. "I suppose that means he's coming down, and we are to wait here, right?"

"I would think so," Sophie responded. "Why don't we sit down on the swing? My hip is killing me."

"Not your knee?"

"Yes, my knee, too. But now my hip has joined in." She hobbled over to the swing and leaned her cane against the banister.

"What did the doctor say about your hip?"

"I'm walking all catawampus because of the knee, and now it's throwing my hip off-kilter."

"And what does he say to do about that?" Sarah asked, knowing full well that Dr. Waller had recommended a knee replacement.

"He's still pushing for me to become a bionic old lady."

Twenty minutes later, when they were beginning to think they'd been forgotten, the front door opened and a clean-cut young man, obviously freshly showered, stepped out. He carried a large mug of coffee and wore a practiced smile intended to charm. "Sorry about that," he said as if he had just stepped away from a board meeting. "What can I do for you folks?"

"You're Donald, right?"

"Yes. Donald P. Wasserman," he announced proudly. "And who wants to know?"

Sarah introduced herself and Sophie. When she began talking about Max Coleman's death, he lifted his head in a knowing gesture. "Ah, Parker. You're that guy's wife."

"Yes. I'm the wife of Charles Parker, and as you know, my husband has been arrested for the murder of Max Coleman. I'm trying to find out what really happened to Mr. Coleman."

"Who cares? The guy was a jerk."

"Well, I care because my husband didn't kill him. And unless someone finds out who *did*, my husband will go to jail, probably for the rest of his life." Sarah's voice cracked ever so slightly on the last few words. Sophie knew she was trying to be brave and quickly jumped in to help her.

"Won't you sit down here with us and at least listen for a moment?"

Donald looked at the two women hesitantly and then shrugged; he pulled a metal chair closer to the swing and sat down. "Okay, shoot. What do you want to know?"

"The best way to help Charles is to find out who killed Max. Do you have any idea who that might be?"

"Wow! You two really cut to the chase." He took the last gulp of his coffee and set the mug on the porch railing. "If I were going to make a wild guess, I'd say it was the husband of one of the married chicks he ran around with."

"He ran around with married women?"

"You bet he did, and some real dolls they were. There was this one …" he gestured, indicating a buxom figure, but then he dropped his hands and said contritely, "Sorry. Anyway, this one was a gorgeous blond chick but ditzy. Really ditzy."

"You knew her?"

"The guys all hang out over at Barney's Bar & Grill—you know, over on …"

"I know the place," Sarah interjected. She had actually named her dog for that establishment because he had been picked up by the animal shelter while he was raiding Barney's dumpster.

"Do you know the woman's name?"

"Nah. But the bartender might. He seemed to know her. In fact, now that I think about it, he seemed to know the little redhead Max hung out with, too. Talk to him."

"Any other ideas?"

"Larry and I heard Braxton swearing at him one afternoon when most of the other guys were gone. It sounded like it was coming to blows, but old Larry and I hightailed it out of there."

"Did you hear what they were arguing about?"

"Something about the inspector; that's all I heard before we left."

"Can you think of anyone else?"

"The guy fought with everybody. He'd have cursing matches with his crew, truckers bringing in supplies, and even the inspector when he'd drop by just doing his job."

On their way home, Sarah and Sophie speculated about the possibility that Max had been killed by one of the husbands of his various girlfriends.

"A crime of passion. A husband in a jealous rage. It works for me," Sophie suggested.

"We'll plan a trip to Barney's and talk with the bartender."

Chapter 25

"We've had a bit of good news today," Charles said as Sarah came in from having coffee with Sophie. "We need good news," she responded. "What is it?"

"Graham called. He and his investigator have been nosing around, and they've learned that the witnesses that said I threatened Max have recanted."

"Recanted?" Sarah repeated innocently, hoping his attorney hadn't revealed the true source of his information. She and Sophie had taken everything they had to him the previous day and swore him to secrecy.

"They said Max had threatened me if I ever came back on the jobsite, and that part is true. And they said that all the other things that were said were said after I left. One guy remembers Max saying, 'If Parker comes back, he's a dead man.' No one could remember any threat I had made other than that I would contact the authorities."

"This should really help you, Charles. Will they drop the charges?"

"Oh no. They still have the fingerprints, and they might not believe this new information. They'll have to investigate whether these guys are recanting under some sort of pressure."

"Is that possible?"

"Unlikely."

"I see," she said naively, picking up her handwork project.

* * * * *

"I'm sorry, Det. Parker. Really sorry. I'm acting under orders; you know how that is," the officer said contritely, clearly embarrassed. He handed the search warrant to Charles and motioned for the other officers to enter the house. "What are you looking for?" Charles demanded.

"Please, sir. Just sit down and let us do our job."

Charles grabbed the phone and went into the backyard. He called Sarah on her cell phone. "You thought of something else you want from the store?" she answered, sounding relaxed and happy. He hated to ruin her mood.

"Sarah, the police are searching the house. I just called Graham, and he's on his way. I just wanted you to know before you drive up and see the squad cars." As he was hanging up, two officers came out the back door and headed for the alley, which ran between the rows of houses. "Is the trash can out there?" one asked.

"Yes," Charles responded, trying to hold his temper back. *How many times I've done this very thing over the years*, he thought. He was glad Sarah wasn't home to see their possessions being violated. He'd try to get things picked up before she returned.

The police in the alley walked back past him carrying a large evidence bag. Charles couldn't tell what was in it. "We picked the trash up and put it back in the can," the younger officer called to him.

"Thanks," Charles responded without looking up.

Not long after the officer's left, he heard two cars pulls up. "What now?" he said aloud as anger welled up in his chest. But when he went to the window, he saw Sarah and Graham getting out of their cars and heading toward the house.

"What's going on, Graham?" he demanded as his lawyer entered, following behind Sarah, who looked dazed.

"They're getting uncomfortable with the circumstantial evidence. They had a warrant to search for something more solid."

"That's a fishing expedition, Graham. You know they can't do that."

"Well they got around it somehow. I have a call in to the detective and the district attorney's office. We should hear something soon."

Sarah looked around the house and was surprised to see everything in order. "I thought they trashed the house when they did these searches. At least they do on television."

"I think they were careful out of respect," Charles responded, although he had picked up the few things they had left scattered around.

They sat at the kitchen table for a half hour having coffee while they speculated on what had been taken from the trash can. "Did they take anything else?"

"I was out back. I don't know what else they might have taken, but both computers are gone."

Charles had looked angry when she first came in but was looking despondent now. He didn't have much to say. His face had become gray and his eyes distant.

Over the next few days, his mood didn't improve. Graham had told them the police had taken a blood-soaked towel and it was being analyzed. "We didn't throw away any blood-soaked towels," Sarah had objected, but Graham said they would just have to wait.

Charles was waiting for that other shoe to drop, and it was taking its toll on him. He ate very little and spent most of his time sitting in his chair with the television on but muted. Sarah was unable to engage him in conversation. She tried to reassure him but without success.

"He's depressed, Sarah," Sophie had said. "Get him to the doctor for medication."

"I suggested that, but he just shook his head. The waiting is just too hard on him."

In the late afternoon, the phone rang. It was Graham. "Put him on the line," was all Charles said.

She quickly carried the phone to Charles, who said, "All right," and hung up.

She looked at him as the blood drained from his face. "It's a match. It's Coleman's blood." As if in a trance, he repeated, "The towel in our trash was covered with Coleman's blood." He looked lost and confused. "Graham is on his way over to pick me up."

"Pick you up for what?" she asked, trying to hold back her own hysterics.

"They revoked my bail. He thought I'd prefer to walk into the station on my own instead of having them come get me."

Sarah fell into his arms, and together they sobbed.

Chapter 26

Sarah could hear the phone ringing on the other end, but there was no answer. The machine came on: "Hello. This is the Parker residence. Leave a message at the beep."

"Hello, John. This is Sarah, your father's wife. Your father has serious legal problems, and I need to talk with you about what we can do. Please call …"

Before she could finish, the phone was picked up.

"Hello. This is John Parker."

"Hello, John. It's Sarah. I'm sorry to bother you, but I need your help. Your father has been arrested, and I'm beside myself trying to figure out what to do …"

"Arrested? Arrested for what?" John asked, sounding somewhat impatient.

"For murder, John. He was arrested for murder." The phone line went silent. For a moment, Sarah thought that he had disconnected.

"That's crazy," he finally said. "Dad worked for the police department for thirty years and was never brought up on charges for undue violence, at least not that I know of," he added, realizing he was out of touch with his father for most of those thirty years.

"That's right, and he shouldn't be in jail. He's innocent, John." She tried to remain calm and not get hysterical, at least while on the phone with his son. "It's just that since you're an attorney, I thought ..."

"Give me the details, Sarah. I'll see what I can do." Sarah repeated the story as it had occurred over the past few weeks.

"Witnesses?" John asked incredulously. "Witnesses to the murder?"

"Of course not, John. Your father is innocent. They're witnesses to an angry exchange between your father and the man who was murdered. A very angry exchange."

"That's not enough to charge him," John replied.

"Also they have fingerprints on the murder weapon."

"Dad's fingerprints? Well, that's pretty incriminating. Were there other prints?"

"There were other prints: two other sets and one or more that were smudged."

"I'm confused. That's not enough to arrest him! Is there anything else they have?"

Sarah was quiet for a moment, then softly added, "They found a towel in our trash can soaked with the victim's blood."

Again the line went silent. Finally John spoke, saying, "I'll call you back as soon as I get airline reservations. I'll be there as soon as I can get a flight. Tell Dad I'm on my way."

After they hung up, Sarah fell onto the couch and sobbed until there were no tears left. As she began to pull herself together, she found herself wondering if some good was going to come from this horrible situation. Charles' son was on his way to help his father.

Sarah wandered into the sewing room and looked at her oriental fabrics. "I'll make a block until visiting hours at the jail," she said aloud, knowing that the steady hum of her sewing machine would soothe her jangled nerves.

Chapter 27

"Oh, Sarah, I wish you hadn't done that." It was the most animated she had seen Charles since he was arrested. "John hates me as it is; this will destroy any chance of us resolving …"

"John's on his way," Sarah interrupted.

"Here?" Charles responded, his eyes wide with surprise.

"Yes, here. He'll be in late tonight, and Graham is arranging for the two of them to come see you tomorrow."

Charles sat dazed. Graham had arranged for Charles and Sarah to visit in a small visiting room normally used only by attorneys. "Charles' reputation with the department goes a long way," Graham had said. There were no windows, and the room was painted a dull green. There was a table and two chairs; otherwise, the room was empty. The guard stood outside the door most of the time, another concession arranged by Graham.

"I can hardly believe it, Sarah. John's coming here? What did he say when you called him?"

"He asked me to tell him what had happened. I told him the whole story. He listened, and when I was finished, he said, 'Tell Dad I'll be there as soon as I can get a flight.'"

Charles shook his head in amazement. "I never would have expected it. I thought …"

"Just accept that he is here to help you, and let the relationship build from there."

"You're right, Sarah. I won't overthink it." The momentary elation Charles had revealed faded and was replaced by the mounting despair he lived with.

Sarah reached across the table and touched his cheek. "We'll get through this, Charles. You've got to have faith that the system will work."

"I've seen it fail too many times, Sarah. Too many times."

She hated seeing him so despondent and hoped that time spent with John would lift his spirits. When the guard tapped on the door, Sarah knew it was time to leave. They both stood, and he kissed her cheek across the table. "I love you," he said gently. "And thank you for calling John. It was the right thing to do," he added humbly. She smiled and turned to leave.

"Wait," he called out, surprising her. "Would you do me a favor and check on the house? I'd like to know how the boys are doing. There's a guy over there; his name is Larry. See if you can find him and ask about the house."

"I'll do that, Charles. I'll go over tomorrow."

* * * * *

She hadn't seen a picture of John and didn't know how they would recognize one another, but she felt her heart leap when a younger version of Charles stepped off the plane. He looked around, and his eyes locked on hers immediately. She smiled and he hurried over to her.

"Sarah?"

"Yes, John. I'm Sarah, and I certainly know that you're Charles' son. You look so much like him." She felt tears welling up in her eyes. "I'm so glad you're here," she added, feeling embarrassed that her voice had cracked. "I'm sorry, it's just that …"

John wrapped her in a bear hug just as Charles had done so many times. "I know, Sarah. I know. Dad and I have wasted so much time, and to be meeting this way now just doesn't seem right. But I'm glad I'm here."

Sarah wiped her eyes with the handkerchief he handed her as they walked away from the gate. "You have another bag, don't you?" she asked, looking at the briefcase and small bag he was carrying.

"Yes. I wasn't sure how long I'd be here. Donna probably packed more than I'll need; she does that," he added with a chuckle. As they waited at Baggage Pickup, they made light conversation easily. Sarah asked about his son. Little Jimmy, she learned, was five years old and full of spunk. "Always into something," John added with a look of deep love.

After they picked up his bag and made their way to the car, John asked if she would like for him to drive. She accepted, admitting that she was feeling a bit shaky.

"Okay, but you're our copilot. Which way shall I head this classy vehicle?"

Sarah smiled at hearing her Oldsmobile being called *classy*. It was almost twenty years old, but she simply couldn't part with it. It was the first major purchase she made after her husband died, and it had become a symbol of her independence. She had worked to build credit in her own name and was proud to have financed something this expensive all on her own.

Once they were on the highway heading toward Middletown, John spoke tentatively. "I know you must have many questions about me and my brother and why we've been so distant."

Sarah interrupted him. "John, all of that is between you and your father. I'm just happy you're here and hopeful that you can get to know each other as adults. Your father is a fine man, and he loves you."

"My brother and I have been very foolish. We've carried our childhood grudges into adulthood and never really questioned them. I've been thinking about it since Dad called this spring. I've wanted to make it right; I just haven't known how."

"And your brother?"

"David's not in the same place. I've tried to talk with him about it, but he isn't ready. It's not just with Dad, either. David's an angry man, and it comes out all the time. He was angry with me for coming and was angry with his wife for encouraging him to come." John shook his head. "I get the feeling she's about had it with him, and that's a shame. She's good for him."

The two remained quiet for the next few miles, each lost in thought.

"Does Dad have a good lawyer?" John ultimately asked.

"I think so. His name is Graham …"

"Graham Holtz?" John asked with surprise.

"Yes. You know him?"

"Do I ever!" he responded with enthusiasm. "I must have been ten or so when Graham started visiting us. He and I hung out together while dad was working. He's the reason I became a lawyer!"

"No kidding? Well, I think your dad's in good hands."

"You bet he is!" John responded with a smile.

"When can I see Dad?" John asked as they approached the town.

"Take this next exit," Sarah said suddenly, almost missing it. "And turn right at the light." Once they were off the highway and heading toward Cunningham Village, Sarah said, "Graham has the two of you scheduled for a visit with him at 1:00 tomorrow afternoon."

"Not until then? I was hoping to see him in the morning."

"Graham wants to meet with you first. He's coming by the house at 10:00 tomorrow. He'll catch you up from a legal standpoint. All you've gotten from me is the hysterics of a frightened wife."

"Nonsense! You've been excellent. Anyone would be scared; this is no small thing, but we'll get it worked out. We just have to stay positive."

Stay positive … no small thing … we'll get it worked out. The words floated through her mind but didn't settle anywhere. All she wanted to hear was that her husband would be back home and their life would be as it had been. She wondered if it ever would be.

Chapter 28

Sarah hadn't seen the house since she and Charles had stopped by shortly after Max Coleman was killed. The exterior walls were up at that time, as well as trusses for the future roof, but when they stepped inside she couldn't make sense of all the studs, which to her appeared to be placed randomly. Charles had pointed out the rooms and the doorways and explained it would look much different once the interior walls were in. "The rooms are so small," she had exclaimed.

Charles reminded her that she had been in the finished model, and they had been pleased with the size of the rooms. "You'll see once the walls are up," he had assured her.

Sarah had decided to drive over and check out the house early while John was still sleeping. She hoped to be able to go with him later to see Charles.

When she pulled up to the lot, she was amazed to see how much had been done. The small front porch had been added, the windows and doors were in, and—except for the lack of siding—the house appeared to be almost finished from the outside. There was a material covering the outside walls that Charles later told her was housewrap. There was a black material spread on the roof, but the tiles hadn't been laid.

With the windows and doors in place, she was afraid she wouldn't be able to get in. There were no trucks around, so she knew Larry wasn't there yet. The garage was open, so she carefully made her way across the dirt, stepping over scraps of lumber and insulation. The floor to the garage hadn't been poured but, except for a few soda cans and cigarette butts, was uncluttered. She made her way across the gravel and stepped up on the temporary step that had been placed at the entrance to the kitchen. The door was unlocked, and she decided to go on in.

"Who's out there?" a deep voice demanded as she stepped in.

Sarah gasped with surprise.

"Mrs. Parker!" the man said, realizing he had frightened her. "It's me. Larry."

"You scared me half to death, Larry!" she responded with her hand on her heart. "I didn't see your truck, and I thought I was alone. Is it okay to come in?"

"They don't like people walking around on the site once it gets this far along. Insurance stuff, I think. Anyway, no one's here but me. The guys were reassigned up the street to try to bring that house in on time. The people are waiting to move in. I just walked up here to get ready for the electrician. Come on in."

"Charles told me it would be under roof before the winter, and it looks like you made it."

"The roofers are coming here tomorrow. They're up at the Jenson house now. Do you want me to show you around?"

"Yes, please, if you have time. Charles wants to know how things are progressing, and he suggested I see you."

"Tell him I'm keeping a close eye on everything, and it's coming along fine. That's the master bedroom back there." The French doors had been delivered and hung but were covered with paper and tape. As Sarah stepped into the bedroom, she gasped. "The shower is already installed!" It looked strange without walls around it.

"That's all one unit and hard to get in later. The plumbing's in place too. You can see where the sink and toilet will go," he added, pointing to the open pipes.

"When will the walls go in?"

"The drywall will be done once we get all the wiring in. I'm working on that today." Sarah could see the pile of blue electrical boxes. "Say, since you're here," Larry added, "Let me ask you. Where do you want the telephone and cable outlets?"

"Well," she responded as she thought about it. "The bed will be over there, and we'll want a telephone outlet there, for sure. I don't know if we'll want a television in our bedroom …"

"Why don't we install an outlet, and you'll have the option if you decide to. How about over here?" he pointed to an area opposite where Sarah had indicated the bed would be placed.

"Good idea. In fact, let's put one of each in every room except the kitchen and dining room, just in case. On second thought," she added, "maybe a phone in the kitchen."

"Do you want to walk on through the house, and I'll mark the places you want them installed?"

"Great! Charles will be pleased when I tell him we did this."

"How *is* ol' Charlie?" Larry was immediately sorry he had asked. Sarah had been smiling and appeared to be excited about her new home, but when he asked about Charles, her expression changed. She looked lost and alone. He wanted to put his arm around her to comfort her but knew it wasn't right. "I'm sorry, ma'am. I didn't mean to upset you."

"It's not you, Larry. It's just that I'm so worried about him. He's lost hope and is very depressed. I don't think he's eating, and I don't like the way he looks."

"Don't they have doctors there?" he asked, looking concerned.

"Yes, but he refuses to see one. One good thing is that his son has come, and I'm hoping that will raise his spirits."

"The son in Colorado?" Larry asked, looking surprised.

"Charles has talked about him?"

"Sure. He told me all about that. Sad situation there," he added, shaking his head. "I'm glad he's here. That whole thing really worries ol' Charlie."

Sarah was surprised that Larry knew about Charles' family problems. *They are much closer than I realized*, she thought, feeling pleased that Charles had someone to confide in.

Shaking her concerns aside for the moment, she smiled and said, "Let's take a look in the other rooms." She almost laughed at the suggestion. She could see all the rooms from where she was standing since there were only studs between them. Together they walked through the house while she mentally placed furniture and told Larry where to put the outlets. "I'll be putting the couch and chairs over there. I think the television would have to go on that wall, don't you?"

"I agree," Larry said, marking the wall with several letters.

When they finished, they had made their way back to the kitchen. Larry marked the stud where Sarah said she wanted a phone. Sarah looked around at the empty space and wondered if she and Charles would ever live there. Larry noticed the sudden change in her demeanor.

"Don't be sad, ma'am. It'll all work out."

She smiled and said, "Thank you," while gently touching his arm. "Thank you for your kindness to me and to Charles. I know he values your friendship."

Larry dropped his eyes and rubbed the toe of his shoe back and forth across the floor. She smiled, half expecting him to say, "Aw, shucks."

* * * * *

Sarah had been gone longer than she anticipated. As she drove up to her house, she saw that Graham was already there. She had made coffee before she left and hoped that John had poured him a cup. Just as his father would have done, John had not only poured coffee but also made a fresh pot and cooked bacon and eggs for the three of them. Sarah's breakfast was waiting in the warming oven. "Welcome home," he greeted with a big smile as she walked into the kitchen.

The men were relating like old friends, and Sarah could only wish that Charles was sitting at the table laughing with them. After Sarah sat down with her breakfast and coffee, Graham explained that he and Charles had been friends for years. "We met on the racquetball court back in the early seventies. We were young, energetic guys who enjoyed sports, and we connected right away. Charlie had just joined the police department, and I was working as an assistant for a law firm in town. Those were the days!" He looked at John and became more serious. "But we married, had children, racked up debts, worked too much, and forgot how to play." He shook his head regretfully. "Charlie lost his wife to cancer; I lost mine to negligence."

Trying to lighten the mood, John spoke up, saying, "I remember when you used to come over and we'd get a game of football going."

"Oh man, I'd forgotten about that. Your brother David was a phenomenal player. Did he go on to play in school?"

"No. David became very studious. He finished undergraduate school in three years and went on to get his PhD in education. He's principal now at one of the largest high schools in Denver. It's an inner-city school, and he's got his hands full."

"Wow! That's impressive."

The three remained quiet for a while, each lost in their own thoughts and remembrances. Finally Sarah spoke up and asked if they wanted more coffee.

"I'll take a cup, Sarah," Graham responded. "Then I think we need to get down to brass tacks."

Once the men had their fresh cups of coffee, Sarah sat a plate of oatmeal cookies on the table and excused herself, saying that she had some calls to make. "We need you here, Sarah," Graham responded. "You're part of the plan."

"The plan? There's a plan?" Sarah asked, sitting back down.

"You bet," John responded. "I'm not licensed to do legal work in this state, but we've been talking about how I can best help Dad."

Graham spoke up, rather apologetically at first. "Sarah, you know as well as I do that the case against Charles was circumstantial at best. But once they found that bloody towel in your trash can everything changed. What John and I've been talking about is that the one sure way to get Charles off is to find out who murdered Max Coleman."

"I know. Sophie and I've talked about that, too."

"I've told Graham that I'll stay on as long as necessary and work with you to find the killer. The police aren't looking. They think they already have him, and they're dead wrong!"

"Sophie and I have made a few inquiries that I can tell you about, but they haven't really offered any leads."

"We'll go over them together. Another set of eyes is often helpful. Also, I have a friend who works up in the state capital now. He's with the FBI on special assignment. I'll get him involved, too."

Tears came to Sarah's eyes as she reached over and laid her hand on John's. "This is the first time I've felt hopeful in weeks," she said. "Thank you."

"We both love him."

"All three of us love him," Graham added.

Chapter 29

The next few days flew by quickly. John and Graham spent hours at the jail. Charles was looking better, and Sarah attributed it to the fact that John and Graham had involved him in their investigation. The three men talked, speculated, took endless notes, and came up with a list of people who might be able to provide them with leads. Much of their time was spent attempting to figure out how the bloody towel got into the trash can. "And why did it appear there weeks after the murder?" Charles asked. "If someone was going to plant it there to incriminate me, why would they wait so long? That just doesn't make any sense."

Graham shook his head. "It's a conundrum."

Charles laughed and turned to John. "That's his word. I've listened to him talking about conundrums now for forty-some years!"

"Life is filled with conundrums," Graham shrugged. "What can I say?"

Sarah had gone to visit Charles in the evening during regular visiting hours but was letting the men spend their time together during the day. She knew it was revitalizing for

Charles to be working at what he did best, not to mention the many hours he was able to spend with his son.

When he wasn't with Charles and Graham, John met with Sarah and Sophie, identifying tasks to be accomplished and deciding who would do what. It was decided that Sarah and Sophie would approach the bartender at Barney's about the two women they had learned about from Donald. In fact, John agreed that they should be the ones to talk to both of the women and feel them out as to whether the killer might have been one of their husbands or even another boyfriend. "They won't be eager to admit it, so you'll have to be sensitive to their body language and the small cues."

"Women are good at picking up on those things, but we'll stay on our toes," Sarah assured him. Sophie and Sarah agreed that Wednesday afternoon would probably be a good time to go by and see the bartender. "He shouldn't be too busy to talk to us then."

"I'll go meet with the inspector," John said. "Sarah, you have his name, I think?"

"Yes," she responded, picking up Sophie's box of carefully alphabetized 3 × 5 cards. "His name is Kenneth Rawlins. He's in the Code Enforcement Office. Here's his address and phone number."

"I think someone needs to sit down with the builders, B&H. Braxton, is it?" John asked.

"Braxton is one of the owners. Bill Braxton," Sarah responded. "There's also a Ted Harper."

Sophie grabbed the box of cards possessively and pulled out the B&H card. "Here's their card with the address and phone numbers. These next five cards that are coded with B&H have all the other information we have about them."

"Other information?"

"Things other people have said," Sarah quickly clarified, seeing that Sophie was becoming agitated.

"Ah, I see what you mean. It says here that Braxton has an explosive temper, and on this card you wrote about the fight Larry observed between Braxton and Coleman. I'll talk to Larry, too. Where can I find him?"

"Under *L*," Sophie said impatiently. "*L* for Larry."

"I see," John responded, glancing at Sarah as they both pinched in their smiles.

"You can usually find him at the new house early in the morning," Sarah said. "I guess Charles has told you about him; they've become good friends. He'll be happy to meet you."

"And he had an assistant, right?" John asked.

"Yes, Donald," Sarah responded. "Actually, I'd like to know more about him. I don't know why; I just had a funny feeling about him. So arrogant for such a young man and with an undercurrent of anger."

"You talked with him already?" John asked.

"It's all in the cards," Sophie said somewhat indignantly.

John picked up the card box, hesitated a moment, and went to *D*. Sure enough, there was Donald: "Donald P. Wasserman, full-time student and Larry's assistant. Heard argument between Braxton and Coleman. Thinks the husband of one of Coleman's married girlfriends might have murdered him."

"Excellent cards, gals. Very helpful!"

"Thank you," Sophie spoke up proudly. "Now, I've got to get home. I left my friend, Higgy, alone watching his Soaps, which are probably over by now."

"Higgy?" John asked.

"Cornelius Higginbottom. You might have heard of him. He's a famous writer of verses."

Sarah snickered and Sophie shot her a look.

"Don't think I've had the pleasure," John responded, aware there was much more to this story. "But I'd enjoy meeting him sometime."

After Sophie left, John packed up his briefcase and prepared to meet with Graham and Charles. Sophie had left the card box on the kitchen table. "Do you think I could take these along?" he asked.

"Sure, but don't get them out of order. Nothing upsets her more than that, and she originally told me she wanted these so we could shuffle them around and find clues."

John laughed and shook his head. "I love that lady!"

Once everyone was out of the house, Sarah took some time to straighten up the house and change John's bed linens. She put the sheets into the washer and went into the kitchen to plan a few meals and prepare a grocery list.

* * * * *

An hour or so later, Sarah pulled into her driveway and was unloading groceries from the trunk when she noticed an envelope on top of her mailbox. "I already picked up the mail," she said to herself as she walked over and reached for the envelope. It had the shape and feel of a greeting card. "It's not my birthday," she said, still talking to herself and hoping the neighbors weren't listening. She put the two grocery bags down on the counter and used a kitchen knife to slice the envelope open.

Sarah recognized the card as one from the box of all-occasion cards she had brought Sophie from Paris. She had chosen ones that were blank inside since the ones with verses were in French. There was a picture of a man and a woman sitting together on a park bench in a field of flowers. The words "thinking of you" were neatly hand written across the top. She eagerly opened the card, assuming it was from Sophie. Inside, a message had been penned by hand:

I know you're worried about your man,
And you probably want to do what you can,
But until he walks out of that prison gate,
There's not much you can do but wait.

Chapter 30

Sarah introduced herself and Sophie to the bartender at Barney's. It was midafternoon, and there were only three people in the bar: an elderly man sitting at the bar, looking as if he'd already had his quota of alcohol for the day, and a young couple in a back booth clearly attempting to resolve a disagreement.

"I'm Rick," the young bartender responded, wondering why the women were introducing themselves. "What can I get you?"

"Oh, no. We aren't here for drinks. We wanted to talk to you about a couple of women we heard have been in here."

"If this is about your husbands, I don't get mixed up in family feuds. 'What happens at Barney's stays at Barney's,' as they say." He grabbed a towel and began wiping the bar. "Sure you don't want a drink?"

"I'll have something," Sophie spoke up as she pulled herself up onto a bar stool. "How about one of those things that looks like a milkshake."

"I can make you a grasshopper …"

"What's that?" Sophie asked, looking interested.

"Its crème de menthe, cream, mint chocolate chip ice cream, and milk."

Sophie smiled. "I'll have one of those with whipped cream on top," she responded, reaching for her wallet. "But leave out the alcohol."

"Look lady, this ain't no ice cream parlor."

Sarah immediately spoke up. "Could you just give it to her with the alcohol on the side? I really need to talk with you."

Rick didn't look too pleased, but at least this would justify charging the full price for the drink. After he added a generous portion of whipped cream and placed the glass in front of Sophie, he turned to Sarah. "Okay, what is it you want to know?"

"I have some questions about a man named Maxwell Coleman. He's the man who …"

"Oh, I know who Max Coleman was. A real womanizer, and I can say that now since the man's dead. There's no privacy to protect now."

Oh, the complexities of bartender-customer confidentiality, Sarah thought. "I'm trying to find two young women that were involved with him—one a blond and one a redhead."

"I know who you mean, but I'll have to think about how much I can tell you. They're still living, and I'm not sure I should be telling tales on them …" he responded hesitantly.

"He wants some incentive money," Sophie said without looking up from her half-empty glass.

"Oh. Sorry. I didn't think about that." She reached into her purse and pulled out a twenty. He looked at the bill without a reaction. She pulled out another and said, "This is for my friend's drink; keep the change."

Rick took the two bills, and Sarah noticed he slipped them both into his pants pocket without going to the register. "Okay," he began. "I can tell you one thing about them. The blond is in here 'most every night and leaves with a different man now that ol' Max is gone. The redhead's a different story. She comes in once in a while, usually on the weekend. If you come by here on Saturday night around 9:00, you'll probably catch one or maybe both of them."

Sophie slurped the last of her drink and started to get off the barstool. Sarah had remained standing throughout the exchange. As Sophie's foot touched the ground, her bad knee collapsed under her. Sarah grabbed for her and was able to keep her from hitting the floor, although she found herself partially pinned between Sophie and the barstool. The man at the back table jumped up and came over to help get them both back on their feet. "You ladies should watch that drinking at your age," he said as he turned to return to his table.

Sophie started to respond, but Sarah was able to stop her. "We'll see you Saturday," Sarah called to Rick as they were leaving.

"That was embarrassing," Sophie muttered as they reached the car.

* * * * *

When Sarah got Sophie delivered to her door and returned home herself, the phone was ringing.

"Sarah, it's John. I just left Licensing and Inspection. I met with our Mr. Rawlins, and I'm feeling very suspicious. He acts like he's got a lot to hide, and he knew I was picking up on it. As soon as I started asking questions, he got very nervous and cut our visit short."

"Did you leave right away?"

"Yeah. I didn't seem to have a choice. But as I walked past his secretary, I overheard him on the intercom asking her to get Braxton on the phone right away."

"I'm going to call Jackson up at the capital. He's the FBI agent I told you about. I'm asking him to look into B&H and Rawlins. It might even involve the entire Licensing and Inspection Department. I'm guessing Max Coleman got caught in the middle."

And if so, it cost him his life, Sarah thought.

That evening, Sarah entered through the visitor's door at the jail and checked in with the guard. She started to introduce herself, but the man said, "Good evening, Mrs. Parker." She smiled and wondered if it was really a good thing to be well known in this particular venue.

"May I see him?" she asked with a friendly smile, despite the nervousness she always felt when she signed in. She glanced down at her outfit as she read the sign: *No revealing clothing. No sleeves shorter than halfway down the arm. No spandex. No dress or skirt above mid-thigh. No clothing displaying obscene language or gang affiliation.* A second sign reminded visitors to place everything they were carrying into a locker, including purses, wallets, packages, phones, recorders, writing implements, and weapons. She tucked her locker key into the pocket of her loose-fitting, appropriate outfit and proceeded to the door that led into the secured area. The guard met her at the door and let her in. "Thank you," she responded compliantly. She hated being there.

The moment they led Charles into the room, her entire demeanor changed. The smile that crossed her face was immediately reflected on Charles' face as he brightened up at the sight of her. "Sarah. I've missed you."

Visiting times were Friday through Monday evenings, with a depressing break in between. "I wish I could see you more often," she said as she reached across the table to hold his hand. The guards were allowing this exception to the rule regularly now. They talked about the family and John, with Charles initiating the topics. She was hesitant to bring up anything that would cause him grief.

"How about the house?" he asked. She hadn't been there since her initial visit.

"I should go back. I doubt there was much done since I was there last."

"I don't know. The roof is probably on," Charles speculated, "and I was hoping they got the right colors. We changed our minds so often, I'm not sure anymore what color the house will be."

Sarah smiled and reminded him of their final decision. "It's like the model," she said. "Light green siding with white trim and dark green shutters."

"Ah, yes. Well, be sure they got it right."

"I'll check tomorrow," she said. "I've been wanting to take John by, but we haven't had a chance this week."

"How's the investigation going?" he asked, "And are you careful about what you're doing? I'm concerned about you getting in over your head …"

"I'm only doing what John assigns me. And I always take someone with me. A couple of days ago, Sophie and I went to

Barney's and got information about Max's girlfriends. We're going back on Saturday night …"

"Take John with you," Charles interrupted. "I don't want you two there alone with that Saturday night crowd. I've seen them."

"Hmm. I guess that would work. We want the girls to feel free to talk."

"John's one handsome dude," Charles said with a chuckle. "He'll get them talking. In fact, I wonder if he should go by himself."

"I'll ask him," Sarah replied. "Actually, I was feeling a bit uneasy about that part myself."

Charles started to say something, but Sarah interrupted him with a big smile on her face. "Wait! I've got to tell you about Sophie." She proceeded to tell him about the milkshake Sophie had managed to trick the reluctant bartender into making, and how she then slid from the barstool, causing a customer to accuse them both of having too much to drink. It was the first time she had seen Charles laugh in weeks.

The guard indicated that it was time for Sarah to leave. Charles leaned across the table and kissed her. The guard didn't object this time, and they both smiled at him. Sarah mouthed "thank you" as she left the room.

When Sarah walked in the house, Barney enthusiastically greeted her and little Boots leapt around, trying to keep up with her best friend. It made Sarah laugh to see the two together: Barney, a straggly mutt, and Boots, such a well-groomed and neatly coiffed kitten. She stooped down and hugged Barney while scratching Boots' ears. "Do you want to go for a quick walk?" she asked Barney. He began running in circles. Remembering his leash, he bounded toward the kitchen and came back dragging the leash with Boots attached to it and hanging on for dear life by her claws. "Wait, Barney. Let me get Boots loose."

When they returned from their walk, the phone was ringing.

"Mrs. Parker, this is Cornelius Higginbottom calling."

"Cornelius, I'm surprised to hear from you. Please call me Sarah. We're all friends, you know."

"I know. I was just brought up to be more formal than people are these days. Anyway, Sophie wanted me to call you. There's been an accident."

Chapter 31

S arah was frantic as she drove to the hospital. Cornelius said that Sophie had fallen, but beyond that he didn't give her any details, saying instead that she needed to come right away.

Every possible disastrous scenario had gone through her mind. She arrived at the hospital within twenty minutes of Cornelius's call and rushed to the information desk. "I'm here to see Sophie Ward. She was brought in earlier this evening."

The woman clicked here and there on her computer, sighed a few times, and finally said, "Ah, here she is. She hasn't been admitted. You can find her in the Emergency Room. Are you family?"

"Absolutely!" Sarah called over her shoulder as she ran up the hall toward the Emergency Room. She had been to the ER previously but only for minor things. She was shocked when she walked into the waiting room and was faced with total chaos. People were being wheeled in on gurneys and rushed through doors marked "Staff Only." Nurses holding charts were taking down information from patients who were waiting to be treated.

Sarah, trying not to panic, made her way to the desk and pleaded for attention. Finally a nurse turned her way saying, "May I help you?"

"My friend, Sophie. Sophie Ward. Is she okay? What's happened?" Her voice was shaking, but she tried to appear calm. "Is … is she alive?"

"Sophie Ward?" The woman looked surprised. "Of course she's alive. She has a bump on her head." She then chuckled saying, "Quite a character, that Sophie Ward. Are you a relative?"

"I'm a close friend. These people look seriously injured. Are you sure Sophie just has a bump on her head?"

"Oh, your friend wasn't involved in this accident," the nurse said reassuringly. "This was a twenty-car pileup on the interstate. Mrs. Ward got here before that, and she's already been seen by the doctor. She's probably ready to go home, but let me check with the nurse." She made a call and turned to Sarah, saying, "You can go on in. They're keeping her for a while for observation; she may have had a mild concussion. Go through that door and ask the nurse to take you to her."

"Thank you so much," Sarah said, looking relieved and wishing Cornelius hadn't been so cryptic on the phone. He could have saved her a great deal of stress by simply telling her what had happened. She suddenly realized that she still didn't know why Sophie had a bump on her head, but at least she'd been reassured that it wasn't too serious.

As she entered the treatment area, she saw Cornelius standing by one of the cubicles holding his hat and looking worried. The curtains were drawn.

"What happened, Cornelius? You've had me really worried."

"Sorry. She said to call you and have you come right over. That's what I did, and here you are." He smiled, appearing to appreciate his competent handling of Sophie's request.

"Okay, Cornelius. But I still don't know what happened. Sit down over here with me and tell me the whole story from the beginning." It appeared she would have to walk him through it if she was ever going to get any details. "From the beginning," she reiterated.

"Well, I picked her up this morning around 8:30 or maybe closer to 9:00 …"

"Not that far back, Higgy. May I call you Higgy?"

"You might as well," he said, sighing. He was getting used to the loss of his real name.

"Now start with the accident. What happened?"

"Okay. We were at the restaurant. I was helping her up out of her chair. I was reaching for her cane—you know, the sparkly one with all the …"

"Yes, Higgy. I know the one. What happened?"

"Well, I was reaching for it when my hat fell off. It landed on the floor right where Sophie was getting ready to step. I screamed 'Don't step there!' and she sort of—I don't know—lost her balance? Anyway, she came tumbling down and hit her head on the table next to us. She landed on my hat …" he said as he held the hat out for Sarah to see the damage. "I tried to catch her, but I couldn't. It took a bunch of us to get her up and get the hat and cane out from under her."

"How badly is she hurt? The nurse said something about a mild concussion?"

"Yeah. They're watching her now. They took some pictures of her head, scans I think."

"And?"

"And what?" he asked, looking confused.

"What were the results of the tests?" *This is like pulling teeth*, Sarah thought. She still didn't know why Sophie wanted her to come in such a hurry.

"She's fine," he finally responded.

About that time, the curtain opened and two nurses came out shaking their heads. Sarah walked over and peeked in.

"Get me out of here," were Sophie's only words when she saw Sarah. She then turned to Cornelius, who hovered by the door, and said firmly, "Out! We need to do girl talk."

Cornelius nodded and immediately withdrew from the cubicle.

"Close the curtain," Sophie said as soon as he was gone. After impatiently answering Sarah's question, she said, "Just listen a minute. Dr. Waller said I can't be alone for the next forty-eight hours. I need your help."

"Of course! I'll stay with you Sophie. I'd be very happy to …"

"Nope. That's not the question."

"Okay, what *is* the question?"

For one moment, Sarah thought she saw Sophie blush, but she had turned away and Sarah couldn't be sure. "It's just that … well … Higgy offered to stay with me. I didn't know what to do, so I told him to call you."

"This is no problem, Sophie. You don't need for Higgy to stay. I'll be very happy to stay with you. I can come to your house, or you can come to mine …"

"You're missing the point. I *wan*t Higgy to take care of me. I just don't know if he should." She dropped her head, looking something between embarrassed and playful. "What should I do?"

Sarah smiled, knowing just what Sophie was going through. These were the very issues she had struggled with for several years. "What does your heart tell you?" Sarah responded.

"My heart tells me I really care about this silly galoot." ·

"And just because he's taking care of you for a few days doesn't mean you have to do anything you aren't comfortable with."

"True," Sophie responded. "You think it's okay then?"

"I think whatever you decide to do is just fine. And remember, I'm right across the street if you need me."

"Thanks for coming over, kid. You're a good friend," she added with a giggle.

She giggled, Sarah said to herself as she headed for the car. *Sophie actually giggled! Will wonders never cease?*

Sarah didn't get home until nearly midnight. John was waiting in the living room. "Thank goodness you're home! I was worried about you."

"I'm sorry. I was so upset when I left, I didn't think to leave you a note." She told him what had happened and that Sophie was on her way home.

"If they think it might be a concussion, she shouldn't be alone."

"I know. I offered to stay with her, but she's decided to accept Higgy's offer of assistance." She smiled at John and added, "I think she's smitten."

"Good for her! You're never too old for romance."

Sarah looked at this younger version of Charles and realized she had come to love him already. She didn't know if it was simply because he was Charles' son or because he was such a delightful mixture of intelligence, humor, and sensitivity. But whatever it was, she had grown to both care for and respect this young man.

Chapter 32

"I hope you didn't mind going to Barney's without us. Charles really felt it would be better," Sarah said as she was sitting down in the living room with John. He had just returned from a late evening having a drink at Barney's Bar & Grill and keeping an eye on Rick, the bartender, who had promised a signal if either of Max's married girlfriends came in.

"The blond came in not long after I got there," John explained, "and Rick nodded to me as he poured her drink."

"How did you manage to strike up a conversation with her?"

"Easy. I just sauntered up to the bar ..."

"You sauntered?" Sarah repeated with raised eyebrows.

"Well, maybe it didn't look that much like a saunter, but that's what I had in mind. Anyway, as I approached, Rick came over and said, 'Pumpkin, this is my friend John. He wants to talk with you.'"

"Her name is Pumpkin?" Sarah said, again with raised eyebrows.

"No, that's just what she likes to be called. Her name is Gladys. She told me that she hates her name. She said it doesn't fit her personality, and I think she's probably right."

"*Pumpkin* fits better?" Sarah asked with a half smile.

"Absolutely! And whoever told you she's ditzy was right on. She asked why I wanted to talk to her, and I was fairly honest. I told her I was a friend of Max, and I was trying to find out who killed him. After I bought her second drink, I told her I was pretty sure it was somebody's husband since he ran around with married women. She said I was probably right and that he was 'a real snake,' to use her words."

"Were you able to get around to asking about her husband?"

"Didn't need to. She volunteered that her husband was in prison for exactly that! He caught her with a guy and shot him 'dead on the spot,' as she put it."

"Well, that eliminates her husband. Could Pumpkin think of anyone else?"

"She was willing to speculate and seemed to enjoy thinking about who might have killed him. Pumpkin didn't seem to know there had been an arrest, and I didn't tell her. She talked about the redhead. Hates her, probably because she was Pumpkin's competition—at least the one she knew about. Rick said Max had a whole slew of women, but he didn't know any other names."

"Does she know how to reach the redhead?"

"She knew her name; it's Kimberly, but she didn't know how to find her. She said Kimberly hadn't been in since Max's death, and she wondered about that. I confirmed it with Rick. He didn't realize it had been that long, but he said that was probably right. He hadn't seen her in a while."

"So neither Rick nor *the pumpkin* has any idea how to find this Kimberly woman?"

"They didn't know, but Rick pulled some guy over to talk with us. He dated Kimberly for a while back before she was seeing Max. The guy wrote her address down for me."

"And?"

"Well, it was too late to go by tonight, but I'll give it a try tomorrow. It's Saturday, and maybe she'll be home."

"You look tired," Sarah said, noticing the bags under his eyes.

"I am. I'm going to hit the sack after I call Donna. It's still early out there."

"John, thank you for all your help."

"I love him, too, Sarah. I just hope he'll come to believe that someday."

"He already does. He understands completely. I hope the two of you can talk about it someday."

Nodding his agreement, he said, "Good night," and gently kissed her on the cheek.

* * * * *

Sarah taught a four-hour hand-piecing class the next morning. Now that Ruth had the extra space for classrooms, she and Sarah were able to teach at the same time, and Saturday seemed to be the preferred time for most of their customers.

Sarah was reluctant to be teaching with Charles alone and miserable, but there wasn't a thing she could be doing for him right then and teaching kept her mind occupied. Her five students were all experienced with the needle and quickly picked up the techniques she demonstrated. They cut out, marked, and stitched several Dresden Plate blocks that she told them they could use to make a pillow or a small wallhanging.

As soon as the class ended, Sarah pulled out her cell phone and dialed Sophie. Higgy answered the phone and explained with little or no detail that Sophie was *indisposed* at the moment. She left a message with him and moments later the phone rang.

"Sophie! How are you feeling?"

"Never better," was her immediately reply. "We played scrabble until 3:00 a.m. This guy knows lots of words!"

Too bad he doesn't use some of them to improve his verses. "But you're feeling fine?" she said, keeping her thoughts to herself.

"Yes. We're way past the required forty-eight hours, but we've been having a nice time. I think he's going to stay on for a while."

Sarah hesitated but decided not to express an opinion. "Okay. I was just checking on you. I'm at the shop and on my way home. Do you need anything from the store?"

"No. We're going out later." Then, in little more than a whisper, she added, "Can I come over later and talk?"

"You sure can! I'd love that. Pop on over whenever you can. I'm going to work on my Asian quilt this afternoon and will be leaving to see Charles around 6:00."

"I'll see you later," Sophie said and hung up.

I wonder what that's all about. She didn't want to appear overprotective, but she found herself worrying about Sophie. Sarah knew she had more than seventy years of experience in the world but not that much with men. She hadn't dated since her husband of many years died in the nursing home after his decline into Alzheimer's. She wondered what Sophie knew about this Cornelius Higginbottom. *I'll ask her this afternoon*, she decided, *and just hope she doesn't think I'm intruding too much.*

When she got home, John was just pulling up to the curb. "Bad news," he called to her. "They flew the coop."

"What do you mean?" she asked once they were inside.

"The house was totally empty. I knocked, and when there was no answer, I looked in the windows. Nothing. A neighbor came over and told me they moved out suddenly without a word to anyone."

"They just abandoned their house?" Sarah asked, frowning.

"The neighbor told me it's a rental. The owner was out last week getting it ready to rent again. He said there was no forwarding address. They just left."

"What do you think?" Sarah asked.

"They could be perfectly innocent folks who decided to move to another house or even another state. On the other hand, the husband could have murdered Max and disappeared, taking his wife along."

"Do you think …?"

"Sarah, that's total speculation. It wouldn't be my first choice. I'm waiting for a report from Jackson."

"Who's Jackson?" Sarah asked, frowning in an attempt to remember the name.

"He's the FBI agent I told you about who's working up in the state capital. He agreed to look into the Licensing and Inspection Department and their connection to B&H Construction. If I had to, I'd put my money on them."

"How would Max's death fit in with that scenario?"

"My guess is that the department, or maybe just Rawlins, is on the take, and Max got wind of what was going on. He might have tried to put the squeeze on them and get a cut. Maybe he was just talking too much. Even that's just speculation, of course."

"There's something else that bothers me, John. It's that young man, Donald Wasserman. There was definitely something off when Sophie and I talked with him. He seemed full of anger. He said something strange when we told him we were trying to discover who had killed Max Coleman. With dark, cold eyes, he said something like, 'Who cares?' "

"Sounds like something a thoughtless kid might say," John responded.

"Yes, but that was a rather cold remark, considering he knew at that point that my husband was sitting in jail for the murder. He just seemed cold and angry."

"Are you thinking he had something to do with it?"

"Maybe. Maybe not. I just think we shouldn't totally discount him. Have you or Graham talked to him?"

"Graham did. He told Graham the same thing he told you—that it was probably the husband of one of his girlfriends." John took on a more serious look as he thought about it. "Pretty pat answer, actually," he added. "Could have been to throw us off the scent. Okay, I agree. Wasserman needs more attention."

They had a quick lunch, and John left to meet Graham and compare notes. Graham had told Sarah that the prosecution didn't seem to be in any hurry to go to trial and that was fine with him. "It just gives us more time to find the killer," he had said.

Sarah went into her quilting room, pulled her fabric off the shelf, and turned on her machine. "The hum always relaxes me," she told Barney, who was glad to be allowed in the room that had recently been converted into a guest room.

Chapter 33

"Sar-rah," Sophie called as she let herself in. "Are you here?"

"Back here," Sarah responded as Barney jumped up and galloped toward the front door.

Sophie walked down the hall and past the kitchen to join Sarah in the sewing room. "Have a seat on the futon, Sophie. I need to finish this one seam."

"What are you working on?" Sophie hadn't seen the Asian fabrics. When she reached the end of the seam, Sarah spread her finished blocks out for Sophie to see.

"I love the Japanese kimonos. Why do the women wear white makeup?" Sophie asked.

"They are geisha," Sarah responded.

"Geisha?" Sophie responded, looking surprised.

Sarah laughed, knowing just what she was thinking. "Yes, I was surprised too, but a woman in the shop told me about the tradition." She proceeded to tell Sophie the story of how the young girls are trained as professional entertainers and are highly respected for their skills in time-honored Japanese arts.

She went on to show Sophie a picture of the finished quilt and then pulled out the wallhanging she had made from the scraps. "This is for our bedroom in the new house," she said, pointing out the kimono-clad women sitting under a lush cherry tree, the koi, the cranes, and the pagoda.

"That will look beautiful with your bed quilt," Sophie responded, gently running her hand over the delicate quilting. She was speaking softly, and Sarah realized she wasn't quite herself.

"Are you okay?" she asked, sitting down on the futon with her friend.

Sophie sighed. "I'm okay, but I'm confused. I'm just not sure what to do …"

"What is it, Sophie?"

When Sophie didn't respond, Sarah suggested they move into the kitchen. She knew it was always easier to get Sophie to talk when they were in the kitchen enjoying a cup of coffee and a snack. She reached for the coffeepot and poured them each a cup. She chose a variety of cookies from the cookie jar and sat down with Sophie. "Tell me, Sophie. What's going on?"

After a long pause, Sophie sighed deeply. "You've met Cornelius," she began. Sarah was surprised to hear her use his actual name. She waited for Sophie to continue. "Well, you know I've only known him for a few months, and you know he doesn't have much of a career as a 'verse-ologist,' which, by the way, is what he's been calling himself lately," she added with a slight chuckle.

"Anyway, he took really good care of me while I was recovering." Sarah wasn't sure where Sophie was going with this, so she simply nodded, not wanting to interrupt.

"So, anyway …" Sophie seemed to be having trouble getting to the point.

"Just tell me, Sophie. What is it?"

"He wants me to marry him."

"*What?*" Sarah was immediately sorry she had responded so incredulously because she could see Sophie shutting down. "I'm sorry, Sophie. You just surprised me. Please go on and tell me about it."

Sophie took a few cookies off the plate and laid them on her napkin. She got up and poured herself another cup of coffee without responding. "Do you want more?" she asked Sarah.

"Not right now, thanks." Sophie sat back down and fiddled with the cookies and finally took a bite out of one. After a long pause, she sighed again and said, "I don't know what to say about it. He asked me, that's all."

"What did you say?"

"I told him I'd think about it."

"And have you thought about it?" Sarah asked, surprised that Sophie was even considering it. She had known him for such a short time.

"I don't know what to think about it. I was hoping you would help me …" Sophie responded hesitantly.

"Well, I don't know much about Cornelius," Sarah said. "Tell me about him."

"Well," Sophie began. "He lives here in Middletown. Always has. He worked as a bookkeeper for the hosiery factory for thirty-some years." She took a deep breath and continued. "He never married. He took care of his folks until they died a few years ago. They left him their house. That's where he lives now."

"Have you seen his home?" Sarah asked.

"Yes. We went over there last week. It's a typical home of older folks—older than us, I mean," she added with a chuckle. "Heavy drapes, doilies on the chair arms, you know the look …"

"Ah, yes. It's probably decorated just as his mother left it."

"You're right! Anyway, it was neat and clean."

"But tell me more about him. What is *he* like?"

Sophie took a long sip of her coffee and looked contemplative before she answered. Slowly she began, "He's kind. He's considerate. He's … what would you say … maybe a little too passive. A little meek. He would let me walk all over him, you know?" she added, looking at Sarah with a very serious look. "But it's funny … I don't want to. There's something sort of fragile about him …"

"You care about him," Sarah said gently.

"Yes, I do. And another thing. Despite those terrible verses of his, he has a sense of humor. Not the sidesplitting kind, but he can appreciate the funny side of life," Sophie said with a very gentle yet thoughtful look.

Sarah was trying to comprehend a side of Sophie she had never seen. *Could this be the look of Sophie in love?* she wondered.

"You told me he asked you to marry him. What do you think about that?"

"I can't seem to think about it. It seems too soon, and it's something I never gave any thought to in the past. It's not that I planned to *not* get married. It's just something that never crossed my mind one way or the other."

"So, now that you're thinking about it …?"

"I could see where it might be something to consider …"

"Something to consider?"

"Maybe," she responded reluctantly. "One thing I do know for sure. It's much too soon. I hardly know the man … but then," she added with the slightest moisture in her eyes, "on the other hand, I know him very well."

"And you like what you know …" Sarah said.

"Yes. I like what I know."

The two women sat quietly, sipping their coffee. Barney, who had been sleeping on his blanket in the corner, got up, stretched, and lumbered over to Sophie. He laid his head on her knee and yawned.

"Well that about says it all, you scruffy excuse for a pet," Sophie said, scratching his head and slipping the rest of her cookie into his eager mouth.

* * * * *

When the guard led Charles into the interview room, Sarah was pleased to see he looked more like his old self. He greeted her with a broad smile and a gentle kiss. She was sure the time he was spending with John was responsible for this change. Also, she knew he was enjoying being able to contribute to the investigation.

"So I have some news, and Sophie said it was okay to tell you."

"What?" he asked eagerly.

"Cornelius Higginbottom has asked her to marry him."

"*What?*"

"That was exactly my response, but as we talked, I'm beginning to think she just might accept."

"He seemed like sort of a buffoon to me. Was I wrong?"

"I don't really know the man, but I can tell you that Sophie seems to care very deeply for him."

"Well, when I get out of here, I'll see what I can find out about him."

"I think we should stay out of it," Sarah said tenderly. She realized it was the first time he had sounded certain that he would, in fact, be getting out.

Charles reached across the table and squeezed her hand. For one second, she saw a glimmer of the old twinkle in his eye.

Chapter 34

There was a tap on the door, and a distinguished-looking police officer in full uniform entered the interview room. Charles eagerly stood and extended his hand in greeting. "Matt! I was hoping you'd stop by." Turning to his attorney, he said, "Graham, this is Matthew Stokely, my lieutenant when I was with the department. Matt, this is my attorney and friend, Graham Holtz."

Lt. Stokely extended his hand and said, "Glad to finally meet you, Holtz. I've been hearing about your conquests for years now."

"Glad to meet you, too, Lieutenant. I guess we've been on opposite teams most of the time."

"Yeah. We take them off the street; you put them back. It's just the way it works. At least this time we're on the same team. We both want this guy out of here."

The three men sat and went through the verbal exchanges that men seem to need before they get down to business. Once the pecking order had been clearly established, Matt spoke, looking directly at Graham. "I came down to talk to Charlie, but I'm glad you're here, Holtz. You're the one that can run with this information." Turning to Charles, he asked, "Are you aware of what's been going on in the Forensic Lab?"

"No, Matt. I've been out of the loop for some time now. What's the story?"

"We've lost a few cases over the past year due to incompetence in the lab. Inaccurate reports have been coming out of there. There was a major investigation, and they let two of their techs go."

"No kidding," Charles responded, looking interested, but it hadn't occurred to him yet why this was significant. Graham began writing ferociously on his yellow pad. The significance was already evident to him.

Stokely continued. "I checked on the computer and discovered that one of the guys that was let go did the analysis of the bloody towel in your case."

"Did you talk to anyone about this?" Charles asked, suddenly very interested.

"No. It's not my place to get involved in your defense, but here I am getting involved—just not in a way the brass can see." Turning again to Graham, he added, "This is your baby, Holtz. Demand that the evidence be reanalyzed by a competent technician. Let them know you're aware of the discrepancies in the lab and that you're ready to go public with it."

Charles was stunned. "We figured someone planted the towel to incriminate me. Are you suggesting it was all a big mistake?"

"That's what I'm suggesting, but don't get your hopes up. Maybe they didn't foul up on this one."

"And maybe they did," Graham added, looking encouraged. "I'll get right on it."

"Matt," Charles said, standing to shake his lieutenant's hand. "Thanks for this. You're taking a big chance with your career by coming to us with this. I can't begin to tell you how much I appreciate it."

"Nonsense," Stokely replied. "What are friends for? Tell that pretty wife of yours hello," and with that, he turned and left.

Charles and Graham sat mute for a few moments, both shaking their heads in disbelief. "Could it possibly be this easy?" Graham finally said.

"Remember, Matt said not to get our hopes up. But I can't help but reach for that elusive life raft."

"I can't blame you." Standing, Graham added, "I'm out of here. I've got work to do!" Their closing handshake turned into a brief and uncomfortable hug. "Hang in there, friend."

* * * * *

"I'm taking a trip," Sophie announced when Sarah answered the phone.

"A trip?"

"Yes, a trip. Higgy wants to meet Tim, and I thought this would be a great way to get to know Higgy better and find out what my son thinks of him at the same time." Sophie's son, Tim, lived in Alaska, where he had worked on the pipeline since he graduated from high school. The previous year, he had visited his mother and met all her friends. In particular, he met Sarah's daughter, Martha, and they became good friends.

"Martha was hoping to get up there this summer, too."

"Would she want to go with us? We might need a chaperone," she added with a giggle. *Another giggle*, Sarah thought with a smile.

"She'll probably want her own trip, but why don't you give her a call tonight and ask? She just might enjoy that."

"But the reason I'm calling," Sophie continued, "is to ask you if it's okay for me to be away. You know, the investigation and all. Do you think you'll need me? I don't want to ..."

"Sophie! Of course you should go. This investigation isn't totally on our shoulders anymore now that John's here. And I don't think I told you, but he has an FBI agent, Seymour Jackson, working on aspects of the case as well."

"The FBI is involved?" Sophie gasped.

"No. This man is an old friend of John's. He's just checking out B&H and their involvement with the inspector's office. He just happens to be FBI, but that could actually work in our favor. You never know."

"Okay. Sounds good." Sophie sounded somewhat relieved, not wanting to leave Sarah in the lurch.

Picking up on her friend's concerns, Sarah added, "And then there's Graham's investigator. We've got this thing covered, and I'm feeling more positive every day. And so is Charles, I might add."

Sarah smiled to herself as she thought about Charles and her last visit. The old Charles was fighting his way to the surface.

Chapter 35

"What's going on, Graham?" John had just joined Sarah and Charles' lawyer in the kitchen. His hair was wet from the shower, and he was dressed casually in jeans and a tee-shirt. Sarah looked at him, again marveling at how much he looked like his father.

"Coffee's on. Help yourself," she said. There was no longer any pretense of formality between them. They were family.

John poured himself a cup and sat down, grabbing a pastry and devouring half of it before Graham responded. "Well, folks, I wanted to catch you both up on what's been happening. I've managed to get some inside information about the shake-up in the Crime Lab. I'm meeting with the head honcho this afternoon to see if there's any way their problems could be used in Charles' defense."

"Are you hopeful?" Sarah asked.

"Always hopeful, Sarah, but mainly I'm chasing every possible avenue. I was disappointed, however, with Seymour's report."

"Seymour?" Sarah asked, forgetting who he was.

"Jackson," John responded. "My FBI buddy."

"Yes!" she responded. "He was looking into possible foul play between the inspector's office and the builder, right?"

"Right," Graham responded. "And Jackson couldn't find any evidence. He said there had been some complaints regarding substandard materials being used by B&H, but there just wasn't anything linking that to the inspector's office."

"The inspector signed off on those buildings?"

"Yes, but that doesn't prove collusion—just incompetence or simply carelessness. It's not enough to go to court with, but I might be able to slip in references to it. Anything that causes the jury to think about other scenarios is good, even if we can't come forward with the real killer. I'm still hoping we can."

"Yes," Sarah replied. "Where are we on that?"

John spoke up, reiterating where they stood. "Pumpkin's husband is in jail, so he didn't do it. Kimberly and her husband have disappeared and can't be located; Graham's PI is looking for them. As I said the other day, they could have a perfectly good reason for disappearing, or one of them might have killed Max. We may never know. Sam will keep searching."

"Sam?"

"Yes, he's my PI," Graham clarified. "He's been digging up dirt on Max, none of which is helping other than to prove the guy was worthy of killing. I plan to disparage Max's character during the trial just to prove there were many folks out there who might have killed him, even though I can't prove that one did. I just want to plant doubt in the minds of the jury."

"How about Larry's assistant, Donald? Did you find out anything about him?" Sarah asked.

"I did, Sarah, and I wanted to talk with you two about that. It turns out that this Donald guy got the job with B&H in order to spend some time around Braxton. He got assigned to work with Larry, so he didn't have much exposure to Braxton. That's why he quit."

"What was that all about?" Sarah asked with a frown. "I don't understand."

"Braxton has been married several times. This kid, Donald, was the son of one of Braxton's ex-wives."

"Braxton is Donald's father?"

"No, his stepfather. Donald's pretty angry about the way Braxton left his mother. She's struggling to get by with two kids still at home, and here Braxton owns a construction company. Donald was hoping to get Braxton to help his mother or at least catch up on his support payments."

"Did Donald talk to Braxton about it?"

"Yeah, and he's pretty angry. Braxton said his mother could go find herself another meal ticket. The kid's disappointed and very angry. If it had been Braxton that was killed, I'd be looking at this guy. But Donald didn't seem to have anything against Max. At least no more than anyone else. He did say the man was too mean to live."

"Braxton isn't his father, right?"

"No, but he's the father of the other two kids that are still at home."

John had been quietly listening to the story with a contemplative frown. "Sounds like a dead end."

"Yeah."

"Could Braxton have killed Max?" John asked rhetorically. They'd visited that possibility in the past.

"Sure," Graham responded. "But where's the proof? And the only possible motive would be if Max found out about collusion between the inspector's office and B&H. But at this point, I doubt that he would have even cared. He might have even been in on it. It's a conundrum," he added, shaking his head.

Sarah smiled, remembering that Charles had told her that *conundrum* had always been his friend's favorite response when puzzled.

* * * * *

That afternoon, Sarah and Sophie drove to the other end of the Village to see the new house. "Look," Sarah announced with pleasure. "We have a street sign! Sycamore Court. I love it!" Several years ago, Sarah remembered, her dear friend and neighbor, Andy, told her to always keep a positive image in her mind of what she wanted. *Charles and I are going to make our home right here on Sycamore Court*, she told herself now. *I'm going to live in that lovely house over there with my husband for the rest of my days.* Sophie noticed a dreamy smile on her friend's face but decided not to ask.

"Look at your house!" Sophie squealed. "It was nothing but a frame the last time I was here."

"Do you feel like going inside?" Sarah asked.

"Absolutely! I brought my auxiliary cane," she added, holding up her old metal drugstore cane.

"Where's your rhinestone one?" Sarah inquired, looking surprised.

"Too nice to use in the mud," Sophie responded, despite the fact that it hadn't rained for weeks.

Sarah helped her out of the car and insisted that she hold onto Sarah as they walked across the hard, lumpy soil where abandoned building materials were still scattered. The floor of the garage had been poured, and there was a finished step at the kitchen door.

Once inside, Sarah gasped. "The walls! We have walls!"

"You do have walls," Sophie responded sarcastically. "They hold up the roof. Now show me around."

They walked through the kitchen, past the eating area, around the fireplace, and into the living room. "This is adorable!" Sophie exclaimed enthusiastically as she looked around. "Where's my room?"

Sarah laughed and led her through the archway and into the hall running past the bedrooms. "Well, this is the guest room, and you're welcome to stay here, but then we're only a few minutes from your house …"

"Only kidding," Sophie said. "But I could stay here for a few days if I ever wanted to, right?"

"Of course you could." Sophie looked somewhat serious, and Sarah realized she might be thinking about having the knee replacement surgery and wanting reassurance that Sarah would help her. "Any time," she added, giving her friend a modified hug just barely within the limits of what Sophie would allow.

When they went into the master bedroom, Sophie squealed and her mood became exhilarant. "This is wonderful!" She hurried across the room, opened the French doors, and looked out across the back of the house. "Is this where they'll be putting the small patio?"

"We had that removed from the plans. Charles has arranged with a separate contractor to have a large patio built that will run from this doorway over past the kitchen door. That way we can have a table out here and a portable grill." Sarah responded.

"How about Barney?"

"We'll be adding a fence once we go to settlement."

"It's practically finished, isn't it?" Sophie asked.

"It looks like it. I'll try to catch Larry one day this week and get an update from him. I've been reluctant to talk to the builders under the circumstances, especially since they think my husband killed their best foreman."

"Unless they killed him themselves," Sophie responded.

Chapter 36

"Hi, Mom."

"Martha, hi. I've been thinking about you this morning. Are you working today?"

"No. I took the day off, it being Saturday and all," she added with a chuckle. "I'm actually working much less these days, and the company is getting along just fine without my obsessiveness, much to my surprise."

Sarah laughed, knowing it was hard for her daughter to admit that work had taken over her life. "Have you talked with Tim lately?" she asked. Sarah's daughter had become quite enamored with Sophie's son when he visited the previous year, and the feeling was definitely mutual.

"As a matter of fact, that's why I called. Tim wants me to come visit him. We've been trying to figure out when to do it, but I don't want to be away during Charles' trial. Do you have any idea …"

"It's up in the air, Martha. Graham told us to expect it to be in a few weeks. I don't want you to hang around here, honey. Go on to Alaska, and I'll stay in touch with you by phone."

"I don't know, Mom. I'd be worried the whole time. I think we'll just wait. I also wanted to ask you what's going on with Sophie."

"What do you mean?"

"Well," Martha responded, "Sophie called and asked if I wanted to go with her and Higgy to see Tim. I didn't know she was that involved with this Higgy. Higgins? What's his name again?"

"It's Cornelius Higginbottom, but Sophie calls him Higgy. And how involved are they? I don't know how involved *she* is, but I do know that he asked her to marry him."

"What? Marriage already? Didn't they just meet?"

"Well, it's been a few months now—maybe four. It's still very early, but he seems to be quite serious. I'm hoping she'll get to know him better, and I guess she's thinking this trip will help. She wants Timothy's opinion."

"Hmm. Do you think she really wanted me to go with them? I could, but …"

"No, hon. I think you should save your trip until a time you and Tim can be alone and concentrate on getting to know each other. And I think you need to spend time in Alaska. You just might end up living up there …"

"No way!" Martha interrupted. "We've talked about that. He doesn't want to stay in Alaska after he retires, and I sure don't want to live so far away. I want to be here in easy reach of my family."

Sarah smiled, remembering all the years that she and her daughter had been estranged. *Things pass*, she thought, hoping that someday all this would pass as well.

"I just remembered something Timothy told me when he was visiting," Sarah said. "He wants to settle down here in Middletown in order to be here near his mother."

"Yes. That's what he told me as well. He and I agree on that. So you think it's okay for me to tell Sophie I'm not going with them?"

"I think it's more than okay."

That settled, Martha asked about Charles, and Sarah caught her up on all the latest happenings. "It looks like we'll be going to court without an alternative explanation of how Max died. We were hoping to come up with the real killer, but it doesn't look promising."

Since the jail was closed to visitors that night, Sarah and Martha decided to meet for dinner. Martha suggested the lodge on the outskirts of town, but since that was where Charles had proposed to her, Sarah didn't think she could face going there. "How about the French restaurant in town where we ate last time?"

"Perfect!" Martha responded. "I'll pick you up at 6:00."

Chapter 37

A few days later, Sarah woke up and looked at the clock, surprised to see it was after 9:00. She rarely slept that late but knew she needed the sleep since she had been tossing and turning the last few weeks.

The phone rang while she was making coffee.

"Sarah, there's been a development." Sarah's heart sank. What else could go wrong? She carried the phone into the living room and sat down in Charles' chair. Just sitting there sometimes brought her a degree of comfort.

"This doesn't sound good, Graham," she responded.

"It's very good. Extremely good for our side."

"Tell me."

"The blood on the towel in your trash can was not even Max's blood!"

"*What?* How can that be? Whose is it, and why was it in our trash can?"

"The blood has been identified as belonging to a day laborer who comes into the community during the week to do lawn services. He probably just dropped it in your trash because it was handy. He's been arrested several times for minor crimes, so they had his DNA on file."

"How could a mix-up like that happen?" Sarah asked, still reluctant to see how this was going to help her husband.

"Remember we told you that there was a shake-up in the lab and two techs were fired? Well, one of those technicians had done the analysis of the towel. I demanded that it be retested by an unbiased third party. They sent it up to Hamilton. The blood they had previously identified as Maxwell Coleman's blood actually belonged to a Colin Maxwell. A stupid mistake by an incompetent technician!"

"How could they make such a terrible mistake? What was going on in the lab that would allow a mistake like that?" Sarah could feel the anger rising from deep within as she realized that Charles might have been suffering through much of this nightmare simply because of a stupid mistake. His bond had been revoked because of the bloody towel. "How did this happen?" she repeated, her voice raised.

"Drugs mostly. Incompetence. Inexperience. But they've cleaned it up."

"What does this mean for Charles? Will he be released?"

"No, Sarah. They still have the original evidence, which they felt was enough to arrest him. I'd tried for another bond hearing, but I was turned down. They want to keep him until the trial."

"You said this is good news. Do you really believe that?"

"Yes, Sarah. He stands a much better chance now. All of their evidence is circumstantial, and I can fight them in the courtroom on that. It was that dang bloody towel … anyway, this is a relief."

"When will he go to trial?" Sarah asked, not feeling much relief herself.

"This shoots a hole in the state's case, and I don't know what they'll do now. We've been dancing around a trial date. I've requested several postponements hoping we'd find the real killer. It won't surprise me if they ask for one now so they can attempt to dig up more evidence. I was hoping to get him back home at least until the trial. Unfortunately, that's out."

"What can I do?"

"Nothing, dear. John and I and Charles will be meeting to revise our strategy. If you want to be involved in those meetings, I'll arrange it with the warden."

"I'll have to think about that, Graham. Thank you ..." she added hesitantly, trying to keep her voice steady but realizing it sounded shaky. "Thank you for all you're doing for Charles," she added.

"It's my job," he responded.

"It's more than your job," she said. "I know you care about him."

"It's more than my job," he said, his voice catching almost imperceptibly.

Chapter 38

"Now that's not entirely horrible," John said, reading the card Sarah brought in from the mailbox earlier that day.

In just a few weeks, he'll go to trial,
Until that time, it's hard to smile,
I see your light on very late,
You aren't feeling entirely great,
But I wanted you to hear straight from me,
That this'll work out—just wait and see.

"Not entirely," she responded with a weak smile. "But mostly …"

"It rhymes rather well," John said, looking for the positive.

"True."

"And it's encouraging."

"Also true."

"And it made you smile …"

"Even that's true, John. I guess you're right. This is not entirely horrible!"

"And your friend loves him. Or as you put it, 'she's smitten.'"

"She's smitten, for sure. I just hope she manages to get to know him better before she does anything permanent."

"Nothing is really permanent anymore," John responded, looking disheartened.

Turning her attention to him, she asked, "What's going on, John?"

"It's my brother, David. I called him and tried to convince him to come for the trial. He's just so angry. Not just with Dad but with life in general. He's angry with me now for staying so long, but I told him I'm sticking with Dad throughout this. David and I've never had much of a relationship, but I think this pretty well finishes it off. He told me not to call again."

"I'm sorry, John," Sarah responded sympathetically. "Do you think you should go home?"

"Absolutely not! I'm here for you and Dad, and it feels right. My wife understands completely."

"Donna's been really good about you being here so long. I'm eager to meet her."

"You will. You and Dad are visiting us for the holidays!"

Positive thinking, Sarah pondered. *Picture it the way you want it to be.*

* * * * *

It was finally visiting day again. Sarah dressed carefully and put on makeup in an attempt to hide the fact that she hadn't been sleeping. Graham had called and said the trial date had been set for 9:00 on Monday morning, just a little over two weeks away. They were all tense in anticipation. Sarah couldn't imagine what this was like for Charles.

When they brought him into their visiting room, he was smiling, but it wasn't the smile he had before this ordeal. That smile came from his soul, and this one seemed to be forced, almost not belonging to him.

"Charles," she said, reaching out her hands across the table even before he sat down. He took both her hands and leaned over to kiss her gently on the lips. "I love you," she said just as gently.

"I love you, too," he responded, but it wasn't the voice she was accustomed to. "I'm sorry to be putting you through all this, my love," he added softly. "So sorry." He dropped his head and stared down at the table. "I'll bet you wish you never …"

"Charles, please! Don't even say it! We've got to stay positive and hopeful. You are going to beat this thing. You didn't do anything wrong, and they'll realize that once we get to court. Have you decided whether to testify?"

"No decision to make. Of course I will. I have nothing to hide, and I want my side out there."

"They'll ask about the towel."

"And Graham will object. It wasn't Max's blood, and I know nothing about a bloody towel."

"They'll ask about the fingerprints."

"I know, and I'll tell them exactly what happened. I was helping my friend, Larry. They're going to call Larry, too, and he'll tell them as well."

"Donald's prints are on the wrench, too," Sarah offered. "Will he be on the stand?"

"Donald's a good guy. He used the wrench every day. Graham wants to insinuate that he had something to do with the murder. I've objected to that. He's just a kid."

"Charles, don't fight Graham. Let him do whatever he feels he should to get you back home."

"I know," he said, again dropping his head.

Attempting to raise her husband's spirits, Sarah told him about her visit with Sophie to see the house. She saw him lighten up when she told him about all the progress.

"Have they painted inside?"

"I think that's probably next. They have blue tape on the windows."

"And the appliances?"

"They're all in and just what we ordered. We're going to love our new home," she added with a confident smile.

He gave her a patient smile and simply said, "My wife. Always positive. Always with that half-full glass." *Mine's not half-empty*, he thought, but didn't say it. *There's hardly a drop left in it.*

Chapter 39

T he next two weeks passed very slowly. Graham and John met with Charles most days working on trial strategy. Sarah decided not to attend those meetings but to keep her visits with Charles just for the two of them (and whatever guard was assigned to watch over them).

It was Friday evening. "Only two days to go," Sarah told herself aloud. Barney's ears shot up. He looked at her eagerly but decided she wasn't offering any of his favorite things: a walk, a treat, a meal. He laid back down and sighed. Boots jumped up on Sarah's lap and purred as Sarah gently stroked her silky back.

Sarah jumped when the phone rang, scaring Boots, who jumped off and made her unthreatening kitty growl.

"Sarah, are you sitting down?"

"Graham, what is it?"

"Sit down and I'll tell you."

Sighing, she carried the phone into the living room and sat down in Charles' favorite chair. "Okay, I'm sitting. Talk to me, Graham."

"Well, I have good news. Actually, it's the very best news we could ever have."

"Graham, quit stalling. Tell me your news. Have you found out something encouraging?"

"Better than that," he said, still drawing out the drama. Sarah was beginning to get irritated.

"Out with it, Graham, or I'm hanging up."

"I'm on my way to your house …"

"Yes?" she responded.

"… and I'm bringing Charles with me."

"*What?* You're bringing Charles? You have Charles *with* you?" she gasped. "Why? What's happened?"

"The district attorney dropped the charges, and the judge released him!"

Trying to pull herself together, Sarah wiped tears from her face with trembling hands and asked, "Why did they drop the charges? How …?"

"They dropped the charges as soon as they confirmed they had the *real* killer in custody."

"*The real killer?* Who? How did they …?"

"You'll get all the details in about fifteen minutes. We're on our way now. I'd put Charles on the phone, but he says he wants to be holding you when he says hello as a free man."

"Can you at least tell me how you caught the killer?" Sarah pleaded, still confused by what was going on.

"We didn't. He walked into the police station and confessed. We'll tell you all about it when we get there. Just relax …"

"*Relax?* You've got to be kidding!" Sarah responded, not sure whether to laugh or cry. "Oh, Graham," she added. "Just bring my husband home!"

Dazed, Sarah hung up the phone, sobbing with happiness this time.

Ten minutes later she saw the car coming up the street, and she ran to meet it. Charles jumped out of the car before it had stopped, and they fell into each other's arms. They laughed and they cried and they held each other. "It's over, sweetheart. It's over."

As they were walking toward the door in each other's arms, John screeched up to the curb in his rental car and hurried toward his dad and Sarah. "I heard, and I can hardly believe it," he gasped. They each reached out to pull him into their embrace.

"Come on in, and I'll tell you the whole story," Graham said. "In fact, I can show you part of the story. I have the killer's confession on tape."

"How is that possible?" John asked. "What are you doing with it?"

"I'm his attorney."

"*What?*" Sarah shouted, looking astounded. "You're going to defend the killer?" Turning to Charles, she demanded, "What's this all about, Charles?" But Graham responded before Charles had a chance to speak.

"I'm defending him because your husband asked me to, and he's paying the bill, so what could I say?" He sent Charles a knowing smile.

Sarah flopped down on the couch and held her head. "You're paying to defend Max's killer? Please just tell me what's going on here."

Charles quickly sat down beside her and pulled her close to him. "It's okay, sweetie. We'll explain the whole thing."

"Let's just watch the tape," Graham said, sliding the disk into the player and clicking on the monitor.

As the monitor came alive, Sarah gasped. "That's Larry!" Recognizing the interview room in the background, she added, "What's Larry doing in the police station?"

"Just watch, sweetheart. Just watch." Charles pulled her closer as all eyes were glued to the screen.

"My name is Larry Jacob Dunkin, and I work for B&H Construction. I was told to tell my story from the beginning, and I'll do that. But first I want to apologize to the people I care about. I've done the worst thing a man can do. I've allowed a good friend and a fine man to sit in jail for a crime I committed. I've hurt him and his fine family, and I can never repay them for that.

"The truth is, I never expected you folks to arrest ol' Charlie, and when you did, I was sure you wouldn't hold him. I thought you'd know right away he couldn't do something like that. Of course, I didn't think I could have either."

He hung his head in despair. After a period of silence, a voice in the background said, "Go on, Mr. Dunkin."

"Sorry. It all happened so fast. I was down in the crawl space doing some adjustments on the wiring. They were above me on the main floor. I don't think they knew I was there. They were yelling and cursing about some shortages or something. Rawlins, that's the city inspector, kept saying he wasn't going to take the fall. Braxton, that's the owner of B&H, he said they had a deal. They both told Max he was ruining them. They cursed and yelled at Max that he was responsible for some investigation that was going on. I didn't understand most of what they was talkin' about. I just went on with my work kind of quiet like. And yeah, I was listening. It wasn't any of my business, but I was listening.

"Finally, Braxton slammed out and Rawlins followed him. They was both still yelling and cussing up a storm. I didn't realize Max was drinking until he walked past the door to the crawl space and saw me. He had a half-empty bottle in his hand. 'What the hell are you doing here?' he yelled. I told him I was working, but he kept on yelling. He said stuff I don't wanna repeat. He was cussing and slamming around, and he accused me of trying to get something on him so I could get his job. Fact is I wouldn't have his job.

"Anyway, he turned the bottle up and drank most of what was left in it. He threw the bottle at me and yelled, 'Get out!' The bottle missed me, but he came at me. He shoved me against the wall and kicked me. Okay. I'll admit it. I got mad. I don't take that from any man. Once I got up, I hauled off and socked him in the face. He went down.

"I figured I should get out of there, and I headed toward the door. I was going to go get my toolbox since I figured I'd probably find myself out of a job the next day. Anyway, I'm walking toward the door and he comes up behind me and grabs me by the neck. I swung around and grabbed the first thing I could reach in my tool belt. It was my stillson pipe wrench. I swung it at him and he went down again. I yelled, 'Never lay a hand on me again,' and I stormed out to my truck and drove home. I realized I left the wrench, but I didn't want to go back. I figured one of my buddies would get it for me if Max fired me.

"I didn't know he was dead until the next day. I panicked when I heard. I didn't know what to do. I knew I should go in and talk to the cops, but I figured they'd never find out who did it. Everybody hated the guy, so I just laid low and went on in to work like usual.

"The worst part for me came when they arrested Charlie Parker. I should have gone right in and confessed then, but I didn't think they'd keep an ex-cop. And besides, he was innocent. I knew they'd figure that out. So I just waited.

"But since then, I got to know the wife and his son, and I knew what I had to do. They were in pain because of me, and they said poor ol' Charlie was suffering in that cell.

"I'm here to tell you that I'm the one that killed Maxwell Coleman. I ain't sorry he's dead, but I'm sorry ol' Charlie had to spend all that time in jail. I know I don't deserve it, but I hope he'll forgive me someday.

"That's about all I have to say. Please send Charlie on home to his family."

The room was quiet. No one spoke. No one moved.

Finally, Sarah broke the silence. "What's going to happen to Larry?"

"He'll be okay," Graham responded. "If it goes to trial, I'll argue self-defense. I already spoke with the prosecutor, and he's willing to deal." He then stood and walked into the kitchen, giving the family their much-needed privacy.

Sarah laid her head on Charles' chest. A tear ran down her cheek and onto his shirt. "I'm glad you're paying for Graham to represent him. Larry's a good man."

"A good man who made some very bad decisions," Charles responded, shaking his head.

"Haven't we all?" John added as he walked toward the kitchen to join Graham. "Haven't we all."

STITCHED TOGETHER

See full quilt on back cover.

Anna encouraged Sarah to make this 25″ × 32″ quilt from Asian-inspired fabrics. Fussy cut your favorite panels, and you'll have a quilt in no time!

MATERIALS

Focus fabric: Approximately 1 yard, depending on panel placement and size

Black: ¾ yard (¼ *each* for sashing, border, and binding)

Backing: 1 yard

Batting: 33″ × 40″

Tip ‖ *Fussy cutting* is cutting around a design. Add ¼″ on all sides for the seam allowances.

Tip ‖ Your panels may be a different size than Sarah's. Audition them on a design wall to come up with the best arrangement.

Project Instructions

Seam allowances are ¼".

FUSSY CUT THE PANELS AND ADD THE SASHING

1. Fussy cut the panels as desired.

2. Measure each panel through the middle. Cut the sashing 1½" wide × the measured width and 1½" wide × the measured length.

3. Sew the sashing to the panels following the quilt image; then sew the panels together. Press after each addition.

MAKE THE BORDERS AND ASSEMBLE THE QUILT

1. Measure the quilt length across the middle of the quilt. Cut 2 outer border strips 3" × the measured length. Add these borders to the sides of the quilt. Press.

2. Measure the quilt width across the middle of the quilt. Cut 2 outer border strips 3" × the measured width. Add these borders to the top and bottom. Press.

3. Layer the pieced top with the batting and backing. Quilt and bind as desired.

Turn the page for a preview - →
of the next book in A Quilting Cozy series.

2nd edition includes instructions to make the featured quilt

Moon Over the Mountain

a quilting cozy

Carol Dean Jones

Preview of *Moon Over the Mountain*

"Another retreat?" Sophie asked. "Is this one on a boat?"
"It was a ship, Sophie, not a boat. But this one is in the mountains," Sarah responded, opening the magazine to the page she had marked. "It's this one," she added, pointing to a picture of a log cabin lodge and a group of women on the front porch proudly holding up their quilts.

Sarah slipped her reading glasses on and read the article aloud. "Quilting in the Great Smoky Mountains. Go back to a simpler time and enjoy the tranquility of the mountains as you learn about southern Appalachian culture while making a memory quilt. Relax on the porch, enjoying the spectacular mountain setting, or hike with local guides along the streams and through the forests to breathtaking scenic spots rarely seen by outsiders. Learn about mountain arts and crafts from local artisans while creating a quilt to display your fondest memories."

"So, Sophie. How about it? Do you want to go with me?" Sophie was Sarah's best friend, a short, rotund woman with an infectious laugh and the best friend a person could have.

"Me? I don't quilt. For that matter, I don't hike. I *do* sit on the porch and relax … but I can do that right here."

"So you don't want to go with me?"

"Well," Sophie began, sitting down at the table and picking up her third donut, "I'd probably go with you if it weren't for Higgy. He wants me to go to Alaska with him in the spring so he can meet Timmy, and I'd better save my traveling energy for that." The previous year, Sophie met Higgy, who described himself as a creative card consultant, although she later learned this was a major exaggeration. Higgy's real name was Cornelius Higginbottom, but Sophie announced that his name had entirely too many syllables for her taste, so she coined him Higgy.

"I can see that," Sarah responded. She knew Higgy was interested in becoming much more serious with her friend, and meeting Sophie's son was a good way to move that process forward. "If you change your mind, I'm sure I can get you in. Just let me know. You won't have to quilt; I promise."

Leaving Sophie's house, Sarah looked across the street and saw her previous home, now empty and with a *For Sale* sign in the small front lawn. She felt a moment of nostalgia, remembering all the times she and Sophie had scurried back and forth between their homes. Sarah and Charles now lived in their new house on the other side of the Village.

As she walked to the corner and headed up the street to her home in The Knolls, Sarah smiled to herself, remembering all the adjustments she and her new husband had made as they struggled with being newlyweds at their age. In their seventies, it was no easy task getting beyond their own habits and preferences. They were settled now and both wondered, in retrospect, why it had been so difficult.

Within minutes, Sarah was turning into Sycamore Court and heading toward her new home at the head of the cul-de-sac. When they got married the previous year, they had lived in Sarah's small attached house across from Sophie, but after a few months of needing more personal space, they decided to purchase a new house in their retirement community.

As she approached the front door, she smiled to realize how warm and inviting their home looked. The Village landscaper had offered a tree in front of each house and azaleas along the foundation. Charles left the choice up to her, and she chose a maple tree and coral azaleas. There was a small front porch with a railing where she added a long flower box, filled now with chrysanthemums since her summer flowers had faded and the days had become cooler.

"I'm home," she called out as she stepped into the living room. She was both surprised and pleased to find the front door unlocked. Cunningham Village had a security fence and security guards who patrolled the streets and manned the entry kiosk. She always felt safe there, but her husband, Charles, was a retired police officer and couldn't seem to set his suspicions aside. When they first met, he had insisted that she lock her door even when she walked her dog, Barney, on her own block. She hoped this unlocked door meant he was beginning to relax and let go of some of his law-enforcement habits.

"I'm back here," he hollered from the backyard. "How is Sophie doing?" Over the previous winter, after years of encouragement from her physicians and her friends, Sophie finally agreed to have her much-needed knee replacement. Despite her predictions of a catastrophic outcome, she sailed through the surgery and within a day was walking with the assistance of a walker and Higgy.

Cornelius, now called Higgy by all of Sophie's friends, moved into Sophie's guest room in order to take care of her for several weeks following her surgery and only recently moved back to his own house on the other side of Middletown.

"Health wise, she's doing great, but I think she misses Higgy. She enjoyed having him around." Barney got up and walked over to Sarah, pushing his head against her in greeting. *He's beginning to show his age*, she thought but didn't say. She had no idea how old he was when she got him from the pound, but the vet suggested he was perhaps seven or eight at the time. Charles was sitting on the ground next to Barney's doghouse adjusting the siding strips he had added to match their own house.

Barney returned to Charles' side, watching but not looking pleased. He had made it very clear that he neither needed nor wanted a doghouse. From the day Sarah brought him home, he had slept in his own bed in Sarah's room. He had reluctantly made one concession when she married Charles; he agreed to have his bed moved into the guest room. But as far as being outside in a green box, well, that was totally out of the question.

"I thought he asked her to marry him. What happened with that?" Charles asked, still mulling over the issue of Sophie and Higgy.

"She still hasn't answered him."

"He's waited over six months for an answer." he responded skeptically.

"You did, too," Sarah reminded him with a flirtatious smile.

"You're right; I did. Well, I suggest she give him an answer before this famous wordsmith gets away," he said sarcastically. In fact, Cornelius Higginbottom was the worst writer of verse the world had ever seen. "What did you do with that terrible card he attached to Sophie's housewarming gift, something about a new house and a frisky mouse …?"

"I put it in our wedding album along with the newspaper clippings about your arrest last year," she responded mischievously.

"Good. They go well together. Anyway, back to the topic at hand. Do you think she'll ever marry him?"

"I honestly can't read her on this one. My guess is that she'll eventually break down and at least give him an answer, but I wouldn't venture to guess what that answer might be."

* * * * *

"Sarah, this looks like such fun! I wish I could go with you." Sarah had taken her quilting magazine into the quilt shop Running Stitches, where she first learned to quilt and now occasionally taught classes. Ruth, the owner, read through the entire article and looked at the brochures and registration forms Sarah had received from the agent. "I went to a retreat in El Paso with these folks a few years ago, and it was terrific."

"It looks like they use local artisans," Sarah said, looking back through the brochure.

"They do. In El Paso, they had Native Americans from local reservations do the demonstrations."

"Quilting demonstrations?" Sarah asked, sounding surprised.

"No, this wasn't a quilt retreat. It was a Native American crafts retreat. Artisans from several Pueblo reservations brought in beautiful beaded jewelry and demonstrated how they were made. Others brought examples of paintings, pottery, woven textiles, and baskets. They even had a woman who came and taught us how to make a coiled basket using willow twigs and yucca. In fact," she added, pointing across the room to a small colorful basket on the shelf behind the cash register, "I made that basket while I was there."

"It's beautiful, Ruth. I think I should learn more about the kinds of retreats they offer. I'd like to find something that Charles and I could attend together someday."

Sarah and Ruth continued to chat as Ruth straightened the bolts of fabric that had become jumbled during the sale the previous day. Sarah pulled together a group of fat quarters for a quick lap quilt she was planning as a gift for Sophie. Inspired by Ruth's basket, she found herself choosing southwestern-inspired fabrics in bold shades of coral, turquoise, and yellow.

"How's your friend doing?" Ruth asked, knowing what Sarah had been through getting Sophie to follow through once she half-heartedly agreed to the knee replacement.

"What a trooper!" Sarah responded. "After all that, she did beautifully and is walking now without her cane."

"That's fantastic. Give her my best. Now, back to this retreat," Ruth began. "Do you know what you'll be working on?"

"I don't know anything about it yet, but it's called a *memory quilt*, and we'll be using some of our favorite photographs. That's all I've been told so far."

"I'll bet they're going to print them out on fabric for you so you can use them in your quilt. That'll be interesting. I'm eager to hear about it."

"I wonder if it might be something we can do here in the shop. Maybe a new class?" Sarah said, looking thoughtful.

Ruth smiled, remembering how difficult it had been to get Sarah to teach her first class. But once she overcame her fears, she had become the shop's most in-demand instructor. "Sounds like a good idea," Ruth responded with her arm around Sarah's shoulder.

As Sarah drove past Sophie's house on her way home, she saw Higgy's new SUV pull up in front. Sarah smiled as she thought about him going out to buy a car specifically for transporting Sophie after her surgery. The flamboyant Sophie, of course, insisted on flaming metallic red.

Higgy had whispered to Sarah in an apologetic tone that it was much too flashy for his taste. Smiling, he added, "but whatever my girl wants."

A Note
from the Author

I hope you enjoyed *Stitched Together* as much as I enjoyed writing it. This is the fifth book in A Quilting Cozy series and is followed by *Moon Over the Mountain*, which takes place in the spectacular Appalachian Mountains, where Sarah divides her time between her quilt retreat and helping an abandoned family of mountain children struggling to survive alone.

On page 220, I have included a preview to *Moon Over the Mountain* so that you can get an idea of what our cast of characters will be involved in next.

Please let me know how you are enjoying this series. I love hearing from my readers and encourage you to contact me on my blog or send me an email.

Best wishes,

Carol Dean Jones
caroldeanjones.com
quiltingcozy@gmail.com